Psalms
139:17

Masterpieces of The Master

The Master longs to showcase YOU
Why keep Him waiting?

DOLLYS Y CROOKS

authorHOUSE®

AuthorHouse™
1663 Liberty Drive
Bloomington, IN 47403
www.authorhouse.com
Phone: 1 (800) 839-8640

© 2015 Dollys Y Crooks. All rights reserved.

No part of this book may be reproduced, stored in a retrieval system, or transmitted by any means without the written permission of the author.

Published by AuthorHouse   10/12/2015

ISBN: 978-1-5049-5571-3 (sc)
ISBN: 978-1-5049-5572-0 (e)

Second Edition (Expanded), 2015
First published by Media Publishing, Nassau, The Bahamas 2007

Print information available on the last page.

Any people depicted in stock imagery provided by Thinkstock are models, and such images are being used for illustrative purposes only. Certain stock imagery © Thinkstock.

This book is printed on acid-free paper.

Because of the dynamic nature of the Internet, any web addresses or links contained in this book may have changed since publication and may no longer be valid. The views expressed in this work are solely those of the author and do not necessarily reflect the views of the publisher, and the publisher hereby disclaims any responsibility for them.

Scripture quotations marked NKJV are taken from the Holy Bible: New King James Version, Copyright © 1982 by Thomas Nelson, Inc. Used by permission. All rights reserved.

Dedication

To my Master – now and forever!
To my pastor, Chris Gill, for showing me
the true heart of a servant of God!
And
For every woman who *has* gone through,
is going through, or *still* has to go through.

Contents

Dedication v

Foreword.. ix

Introduction.. xi

Chapter 1   The Master Calls.................................... 1
Chapter 2   A Prized Possession 17
Chapter 3   When Life Just Doesn't Make Sense 32
Chapter 4   Nightmares Tell a Story 55
Chapter 5   Tenacity under the Sentence of Death....... 72
Chapter 6   As Graceful as a Palm Tree 83
Chapter 7   Don't Mind What He Calls You!.............. 92
Chapter 8   All Cleaned Up!.......................................107
Chapter 9   First, but Still Not Loved 118
Chapter 10 Watch Your Mouth!................................ 127
Chapter 11 Single, but Not Alone 138
Chapter 12 The Master Always Has a Plan!................150

Foreword

The question, "What is truth?" asked by Pilate when Jesus was standing right in front of him, is a question still being asked today centuries later. In this ever-changing and uncertain world, people are craving stability and security, wanting to build their lives on a standard that is unchanging. They are still looking for 'truth'.

This book provides the certainty of biblical truth, sometimes wrapped in a twenty-first-century context, which is both refreshing and life giving.

Chapter by chapter the reader is led into the lives of women whose situation or circumstance has been changed forever by the healing truth of God's touch and presence.

Challenging and heart stirring, this book will appeal to Christians and non-Christians alike. It is my hope and prayer that it produces abundant and lasting fruit for all those who turn its pages.

Chris Gill
Pastor, King's Church Gillingham
June 2015

Introduction

Masterpiece: a work of art,
made with consummate skill,
complete, perfect, and supreme

For a long time I had thought to do a study on the *least* talked about women in the Bible who overcame great sorrow and pain. As I meditated on which character to commence with, Genesis 3: 16 sprang to mind:-

To the woman He (God) said:
"I will greatly multiply your sorrow and your conception; in pain you shall bring forth children; your desire shall be for your husband, and he shall rule over you."

The words *greatly multiply your sorrow* leapt out at me. Ever since the Garden of Eden, women from every culture, creed, and race can identify with these words, experiencing much sorrow as they go about their daily lives. At times, the pain is unbearable, yet down through the eons of time, we see biblical women overcoming these seasons their lives have

Dollys Y Crooks

brought them. That was the essence of my study. How did they do it in light of the above Scripture?

Then I turned to the book of Esther and read where King Ahasuerus was persuaded to sign a decree for the annihilation of the Jews. I read that once a law was written in the king's name and sealed with his ring, it became irrevocable. When Esther, his queen, revealed her Jewish identity to him, although he loved her, he could not reverse his previous law. He could only pass a new one. This new law allowed the Jews to take up arms to defend and protect themselves.

And so it was with Adam. He was given one law to obey: do not eat from the tree of good and evil. Although Eve was tricked into disobeying that law, God too could not revoke the consequences that followed the breaking of it. Instead, because of His love for them, He instigated a new law, *the law of faith!*

One day as I read about Jochebed (Exodus 6: 20), the Holy Spirit whispered, "Turn all you have studied into a book." I laughed. *A book? What do I know about writing a book?* Try as I might, though, I just could not get rid of the thought. Eventually I said, "Lord, I will if You will help me."

As you read this book, you will see the operation of the law of faith in the tapestry of this complex reality we call life. Women, upon hearing a *spoken* word, received it into their hearts as a seed; then, by faith, they believed and cherished it until one day that very *law of faith* produced the changes they so desired.

Have you discovered this new law? You will find that when you put it into action, you will reap great rewards.

I hope you enjoy reading *Masterpieces of The Master* as much as I have enjoyed studying and writing it.

During the course of doing so, I experienced a range of emotions – laughter, sadness, tears, joy, and admiration for these women – as well as reminiscing on my own life and the hardships I too have experienced and by this very law have overcome.

In each story, I marvelled at the Master's ability to create masterpieces out of the pain and trials of life. Am I one of the Master's Masterpieces? A resounding yes!

I have given names to those unnamed in the Bible and changed the real names of the true characters, except of course, the Master's! Since I have created stories around them, I felt I would not have done the Scriptures justice to retain their real names.

Whoever you are, whatever your background, please allow the Master to create a masterpiece out of your life, your wounds, your sorrow, and your pain. Let Him create a tapestry whose outside is beautiful and pleasant to look at – one which, when seen on the reverse, contains many strands of thread, all of different colours and sizes intricately weaving in and out, each telling its own story; everyone a memory, some longing to be forgotten, others fondly remembered. Each strand makes no sense on its own, but together they intertwine to create a work of art at which onlookers simply stand and stare in awe.

But without faith it is impossible to please Him, for he who comes to God must believe that He is, and that He is a rewarder of those who diligently seek Him. (Hebrews 11: 6)

God bless.

A TRIBUTE

To the memory of my mother, the late May-
Elaine Eudora Stewart (nee Singh), a Masterpiece
God unveiled at the tender age of twenty-six.
Mother, in this unveiling you left behind three
strands of the finest silk thread – two girls
and one boy – your tapestry in this wonderful
and complex experience that is called life.
On the outside, we reveal a beautiful picture of you:
your eldest daughter displaying your creativity;
your only son, your beauty; and
I, your second daughter, your personality.
But take a peek on the reverse side, and you will
see the pain and heartache of losing you when we
were so young, of missing you, of having no-one
to turn to except each other, when life got rough.
I have mourned your loss all my life and sought for
many to bridge the gap, only realizing after some
fifty years and more that there is none who can
ever fill such a high and lofty place in my life.
So, Mother, I dedicate the first chapter of this my
first book to your memory – the first Masterpiece
in the lives of three strands of the finest silk thread.
I know that Jesus is the Resurrection and the Life,
and one day we shall hopefully meet with you again.

*"A mother holds her children's hands for a moment,
but their hearts forever!" (Unknown)*

Chapter 1

The Master Calls

She had come to the garden, to the tomb in which they had laid His body, wanting to be near Him. She longed to hear Him call her name again. You see, many men had called her name in her lifetime, but there was something special about the way *He* called her. Was it His distinctive tone – deep, yet gentle – or was it the way He smiled, face wrinkled as He called her with eyes so alive and full of compassion? Suddenly she heard in the softest of whispers, "May-Elaine."

That voice! Instantly, May-Elaine turned towards the direction of the whisper. Recognizing its distinct tone, she could only exclaim with swollen eyes and a tear-stained face, "Rabboni! Master! It is You!"

May-Elaine gathered up her garment and ran towards Him, wanting so much to be near Him. But as she drew close, He stretched forth His hands and with that same gentle voice said, "You can't touch Me now, for I have not yet ascended to the Father. Go and tell My brothers and sisters that I am going to My Father and their Father, to My

Dollys Y Crooks

God and their God. Let them know that they shall see Me again, just as you have."

And with that same wrinkled face and eyes so alive and full of compassion, her Master smiled and vanished, just as suddenly as He had appeared.

•

May-Elaine fell to her knees, cupping her face in her hands. Her encounter with her Master had seemed surreal. Yet there was no doubt in either her heart or her mind that her Master had indeed risen from the dead and had spoken to her. Surrounded by the beauty and peace of the garden and while the morning broke and the birds chirped happily away, May-Elaine mulled over her reason for being in the garden.

•

She remembered how she had pushed her way to the front of the huge crowd and watched Him, His body battered and bloodied under the sheer weight of His cross. Its heaviness caused Him to stoop and stumble several times as He made His way to the place of crucifixion. May-Elaine saw how the crown of thorns placed on His head wove its prickly spikes into the sides of His bruised face, causing droplets of blood to flow down unto His torn and tattered garment. Meanwhile, her heart felt as though it was about to break into tiny pieces.

How she had longed to help Him carry His cross, but she knew she couldn't. It wasn't just her physical strength, but her being a woman also negated this desire. Even in

The Master Calls

the condition He was in, May-Elaine was certain He saw her, for He seemed to smile at her, whisper her name, and gesture through swollen eyes that everything was going to be all right.

Not bearing to look at Him anymore, she turned, pushed her way back through the crowd, and ran as fast as the wind, not caring where it took her, so long as it was far from the scene she had just witnessed. After a while, she found herself on a hill.

"Oh no!" she cried. "This is Golgotha, the place of the skull. It's where He is heading to, to be crucified!"

Hiding away amongst the rocks, May-Elaine sobbed until her tears subsided, and they were no more to be found. She cried for the injustice that had been done to a Man who did only good – one who demonstrated His love for the discarded not only by words but also by His deeds. This Man, for His love of society's poor, was now bearing the stigma and castigation of the Pharisees, the scribes, and the Sadducees – the Jewish religious authorities, whom He had often denounced for their hypocritical ways and pompous ceremonies.

Did not she herself share in this love the time He delivered her personally from seven demons? Demons that had tormented her and dictated her behavioural patterns for most of her adult life? Despite the condition He had found her in, had He not set her, a daughter of Abraham, free from the bondage that had enslaved her? Shuddering at the memory of the person she once was, before He delivered her, May-Elaine preferred to focus instead on how great a debt she owed Him.

Dollys Y Crooks

•

She remembered the day someone had told her of Rabbi Jesus. Some even claimed He was the Messiah and a handsome one at that. From a very young age, May-Elaine had learned about the Messiah (Mashiach), who would be a descendant of King David ruling over Israel and bringing peace to the entire world. She had been taught about Abraham, the father of her nation; of Moses and the Ten Commandments, and of the bravery of Queen Esther when her people were faced with extinction. These were only a few among so many other stories she had been told as a child.

But while her people waited for Messiah's coming, May-Elaine would simply continue to live just as she had always done, confident that, when He came, she would surely hear of the event.

She recalled how according to some, this event had indeed happened. "But how could *He* be the Messiah?" She had reasoned. Her people were still under Roman occupation. There was no peace. Nothing had changed. But wait, if the rumours she had heard of Him and the things He did were true, *then* things had changed. For it was said that He cast out devils, healed the sick, and made the blind see, the deaf hear, the lame walk, and the dumb talk. Why, He even touched and cleansed lepers, making them whole! Healing? Cleansing lepers? Casting out devils? Could this possibly *be* Mashiach?

•

May-Elaine reminisced about the day and the moment her life changed forever. It was the day the Messiah visited

The Master Calls

her city. Throngs of people, most with needs, others merely curious, blocked the streets and gateways just to get a glimpse of Him. Curiosity getting the better of her, May-Elaine decided to see if the rumours about Him were indeed true. Why, she had even heard that some of His followers were women. That was another socio-religious code He had broken.

I wonder how the religious authorities are taking to Him, she had mused. To touch lepers was one thing, but to have women following Him? She wasn't sure which one brought the greater condemnation. All her life she had been taught that a woman's place was in the home, cooking, cleaning, and taking care of her husband and children, not following after a man some were claiming to be the Messiah. To May-Elaine, this Mashiach certainly did not fit the picture she had of a holy man.

She suddenly remembered the rumour that He was eligible and decided to dress in her finest. Would it be possible to gain His attention, despite the throngs of people?

•

Pressing through the avid crowd, being pushed and shoved everywhere, May-Elaine concluded it was all too much. She would wait for another day, when all the fuss about Him had died down and His popularity waned. But as she turned to retrace her steps, something strange yet wonderful happened. In the midst of such a deafening crowd, she had heard a gentle voice say, "May-Elaine."

Surely, it wasn't meant for *her?* There must be countless May-Elaines here. It was a common name among her people. Could He really be calling her? As she turned towards that

Dollys Y Crooks

gentle voice, she could see Him forcefully striding in her direction, the crowds parting with every step He took. Looking so assured of Himself, yet not arrogant in any way, Rabbi Jesus, the one some called Messiah, drew closer and closer still.

May-Elaine stood trembling and powerless, having caught not only the attention of Mashiach but also that of the crowd. Had this not been her intention in the first place?

Wow! He's more handsome than I imagined were the last words she could recall saying to herself when suddenly His voice roared with power and authority. With the motion of a sharp two-edged sword, it severed through May-Elaine's thoughts. "Loose her and let her go!"

Everything around May-Elaine went blank. Regaining consciousness and oblivious to the fact that the huge crowd had drawn even closer, she could only gaze upon the handsome, smiling face of Messiah, so full of compassion, His eyes sparkling with light, life, and laughter. "Daughter, you are made whole," He told her. "Go and sin no more."

•

In the days that followed, May-Elaine struggled to tell of the wonderful change that had occurred deep within her heart – how Messiah's words had pierced her soul, thoroughly washing and cleansing it, and how for the first time in her adult life, she felt good about herself. Her experience was too wonderful for words, yet those who listened and knew her past attested to the drastic change she was so desperately trying to describe. To them, there was no need for words; the change in her lifestyle was proof enough. From now on, May-Elaine would no longer live for herself and her selfish desires. Instead she would live to bring glory and honour to the One who had so marvellously changed her life.

•

How could she, a woman, not become His disciple after what He had done for her? Forgetting her pain, May-Elaine smiled as she thought of life as one of His disciples during those early days. It meant travelling with Him, preparing meals, praying for and with Him, watching the miracles He performed from day to day, and listening attentively as He spoke of God and His kingdom. She had listened as He spoke of His death but then would reassured them that He would rise again.

May-Elaine's life became one of service and testimony to His love and compassion, particularly with regard to the poor and outcast of society. She watched Him many times heal the sick, cleanse the lepers, and open the eyes of the blind. She was there when He brought Richard, Beverley's son, back to life en route to the cemetery, and she was one of the women who ate from the little boy Simon's lunch of five loaves and two fishes.

Meeting Messiah, May-Elaine had concluded, was the best thing that ever happened to her. She needed no one to tell her about Him now for she could personally testify that all she had heard concerning Him was indeed true.

•

For a few years things were good, and His popularity grew out of all proportion. In every city He visited, men, women, children, and non-Jews believed and followed Him.

Dollys Y Crooks

Even some of the religious authorities secretly changed their ways and joined Him too. People were hungry and their needs were great. Some cried out to be fed and to be healed both physically and spiritually. Mothers brought their children for Him to lay His hands upon them and bless them; fathers carried their demon-possessed children for deliverance. Lepers sought cleansing, and still others looked to Him to bring about political change – each seeing Him for what they needed Him to be.

Then one day, her world was shattered. Messiah had been arrested while spending time in prayer with some of His disciples in this same garden she was reminiscing in. Upon hearing the news, May-Elaine reasoned it must have something to do with the Jewish religious authorities who hated Him and wanted Him dead. They had tried several times to get rid of Him but without success. Messiah had told them then that His time had not yet come. Many of them did not understand on those occasions what He had meant by this.

How she had marvelled at His boldness in dealing with the religious authorities. He could read their hearts and was never afraid to expose what He saw in them. He had called them hypocrites to their faces, declaring that outwardly they appeared to be righteous men who upheld the law at every turn, yet they neglected to show God's love and compassion for the poor, instead keeping the people in bondage through their interpretation of Scripture.

Once when reading in the synagogue, having been given the scroll of the prophet Isaiah, He had read:

> The Spirit of the LORD is upon Me, because
> He has anointed Me to preach the gospel

The Master Calls

to the poor; He has sent Me to heal the broken-hearted, to proclaim liberty to the captives and recovery of sight to the blind, to set at liberty those who are oppressed; to proclaim the acceptable year of the LORD.

After reading, He had sat down and announced, "This day is this scripture fulfilled in your ears." Jealousy and envy could only be the reason for His arrest, May-Elaine concluded.

•

Soon she learned that the religious authorities had indeed everything to do with her Master's arrest. After facing two hastily convened Jewish trials, He was charged with blasphemy. He had claimed to be the "Son of God," and under Jewish Law, such a claim brought the death penalty. However, killing Him themselves would defile them, because they were "holy" men of God. Instead they carried Him to Pilate, the Roman governor, and accused Him of being a criminal.

Hurriedly making her way to Gabbatha, the place where prisoners were judged, May-Elaine watched as the crowds swelled. She heard Pilate declare, "I find no fault in this man. I shall release Him!"

Relief swept over her: He was safe after all. Everything would be okay now. But May-Elaine was forgetting that He had often told them how He would die.

Suddenly, the religious authorities stirred up the emotions of the crowd and they began to roar, "Crucify Him! Crucify Him!"

Dollys Y Crooks

May-Elaine was close enough to hear Pilate reply, "You crucify Him!"

To which those who had brought Jesus to him retorted, "We have a law, and by this law He must die because He calls Himself the Son of God. If you let Him go, you are no friend of Caesar's! Anyone who declares himself to be a king is a threat to Caesar, our real king."

Pilate heard this and, fearing that if this state of affairs ever reached Caesar's ears, he himself would be in grave danger, he gave the command to crucify Jesus.

May-Elaine's heart sank. They had caught Him on both religious and political angles. Clasping her hands tightly over her ears trying to shut out the angry voices, she could only look on in dismay as the crowds surged towards Him, soldiers on every side trying in vain to block their way.

"No!" May-Elaine uttered with a piercing shriek. "He hasn't done anything worthy of death. You have the wrong man!" But it was all to no avail. Her screams could not be heard above the frenzy and passion into which the religious authorities had stirred up the people.

Where were all the people He had so tenderly touched, those He had so compassionately healed? Where were those whose dead He brought back to life? Did they not have a voice too? Or were they too afraid to use it? Even worse, were they in this angry crowd yelling for Him to be crucified? Somehow, she found this last thought hard to believe.

•

Sounds of repeated pounding brought May-Elaine back to the present. Emerging from the rocks, she could clearly see Roman soldiers hammering nails into the hands and

The Master Calls

feet of the two thieves. But where was Mashiach? Her heart racing, she searched the hill until eventually her eyes found Him. His cross had not yet been raised. He would be next, the One who had set her free.

"Please don't," she whispered. "Please stop. He doesn't deserve to die like the criminals on His left and right. He is a good man."

Gathering up her robe, now stained with tears, she ran towards the place of crucifixion. *I can't leave Him. He has to know that I am here for Him.* Halfway there, she suddenly stopped. *I can't face it. I can't watch them hammer those cruel nails into His hands and His feet. I can't do it. I just can't.*

Then as though in answer to a question asked by someone unseen, she whispered, "Yes, I do love Him. I love Him very much, and because I do, I can. Yes, I can." Her answer endowing her with strength, May-Elaine silently made her way to the place where they had now raised His cross.

Joining His mother, His aunt, and another disciple, May-Elaine watched as her Master's body hung limply on the cross. A cruel cross that held Him captive as blood streamed unceasingly from His head, His hands, and His feet. His face was so disfigured, she longed to take Him down to comfort Him and to saturate His wounds with ointment and sweet spices.

Drawing close, she heard Him console one of the men crucified beside Him. "Just like You," she whispered. "Even in Your agony, You are still reaching out to those who are hurting. Oh, why are You hanging on that cruel cross? You don't deserve to die like this. If anything, I should be there for all the wrongs I have done. Not You. You have only ever

Dollys Y Crooks

done good deeds. How could You allow them to do this to You? Where is Your Father You spoke of so often? Can He not send His ministering angels to rescue You?"

•

His words, "It is finished. Father, forgive them, for they know not what they do," jolted May-Elaine pulling her back to the awful scene before her. Overcome with grief, she again forgot that He had frequently spoken, particularly recently, of the manner in which He would die. Of course, they had always refused to believe that anything like that could ever happen to Mashiach. Yet it did. Here she was, watching Him die just as He'd said He would.

•

It was the Jewish custom not to allow bodies to remain on the cross on the Sabbath day. As it was the day before Sabbath, the religious authorities requested permission to break the men's legs in order to bring about their deaths more swiftly.

"This one's dead, sir," the Roman soldier remarked. May-Elaine, weighed down by sorrow, upon hearing those words slowly raised her head and looked up just in time to see the soldier standing before her Master. He was dead? How could He have died so soon? She knew from past crucifixions that it took victims quite some time to die. Glancing around, she could see one of the thieves already had his legs broken, and the other was still alive awaiting his turn.

The Master Calls

Focusing her attention once again on Messiah, May-Elaine marvelled at how peaceful He looked even in death. She reminded herself that this was no ordinary man hanging on that middle cross. This was the One who healed the sick and opened blind eyes. This was Messiah!

Feeling a gentle hand upon hers, May-Elaine turned and saw Jennifer, another disciple. "Jabez has gained permission to take His body down," she said softly. "He will place it in the new tomb he has recently constructed for himself in the garden nearby. Let's follow him."

Jabez, a wealthy man, had secretly followed Messiah for fear of the Jewish leaders. But now that Messiah was dead, he felt it a privilege to bury Him in his tomb. After all, he was not quite ready for it as yet. Hand in hand, the women watched as Jabez and a few of the other disciples, as was customary before burial, wrapped Mashiach's body in linen cloths and a mixture of myrrh and aloes. Then after laying His body in the tomb, the men sealed the entrance with a huge stone.

As the day drew to a close, the disciples, exhausted by its events, left the place of their Master's burial with May-Elaine sadly remarking, "Messiah didn't even possess His own tomb. He had to borrow another's."

In their grief, no one remembered Mashiach had said, "I will rise again!"

•

The Sabbath over, May-Elaine shuddered at the thought of His body lying on the cold, stone floor of the tomb. She rose up early, while it was still dark, and made her way to the garden. She needed to be near Him. Her soul ached for

Dollys Y Crooks

Him. But as she arrived at the tomb's entrance, her heart raced. The stone that had sealed the tomb's entrance was gone!

Maybe, she reasoned, *because it is still quite dark, I have come to the wrong tomb. Let me retrace my steps.* Retracing her steps brought her back to the exact spot she was standing before. *This has to be His tomb. But where is He?*

May-Elaine ran from the garden. Gasping and out of breath, she found two other disciples. "They have taken Him away. They have taken His body out of the tomb!" she cried.

Both disciples looked at her puzzled, "What do you mean they have taken Him away? Who has?"

"His tomb is empty. I tell you, it is empty!"

Leaving an astonished May-Elaine behind, the men dashed to the garden, one outrunning the other. Sure enough, the linen cloth that had wrapped Messiah's body and the napkin that covered His head remained in their exact positions as His body had lain. But there was no body – the tomb was empty.

Numb with shock, both men turned to each other in disbelief. They could no longer doubt May-Elaine's words but only ask the same questions: Where is He? Where did He go? Who moved Him? There had to be a logical explanation. Without another word, they headed for the garden's entrance and slowly made their way home.

May-Elaine returned to the garden as they were walking away. Their eyes met, hers pleading: Did you find Him? Shaking their heads in the negative, both men continued on their way. But not May-Elaine; she chose to continue in the opposite direction. She would search for Mashiach, and if anyone had moved His body, she would find it.

The Master Calls

•

Distraught and weeping, she sat at the tomb's entrance. Where was He? Taking one last look inside the tomb, hoping against all odds that her Messiah would suddenly reappear, May-Elaine saw two angels instead, one at the head and the other at the feet where her Master's body should have been.

"Woman, why are you weeping?" They asked in unison.

"Someone has taken my Master's body, and I don't know where they have carried Him," she replied.

Regaining her composure, May-Elaine turned away without waiting for an answer. Suddenly, she noticed a man standing close by and wondered how long he had been there.

"Why are you crying?" the stranger asked gently.

Supposing him to be the gardener, she replied, "Sir, if you have taken Him away, please tell me where, so I can go and bring His body back."

That was the moment when May-Elaine heard Mashiach's distinctive tone – deep, yet gentle – and saw His smile, the one that caused His face to wrinkle and His eyes to shine with compassion, as He called her name once more.

He had *risen!* He was alive. He had overcome death, just as He said He would. That was why He was laid in Jabez's borrowed tomb. It was time to rejoice! Messiah had kept His word.

•

This woman, whose name He called as He delivered and set her free from seven demons, this woman who in gratitude loved Him with all her heart and soul, refused to just accept that He had risen. She wanted to see Him again

Dollys Y Crooks

and through dogged determination, was the first to see and speak with Him *after* His resurrection from the tomb and *before* His ascension to the Father. Did He make a special trip just for her?

•

This story is found in John 20:11–18.
The true characters are Jesus and Mary Magdalene.

•

Have you heard His gentle voice calling your name too? Have you heard Him calling you to a life of service? To lay down your desires, your wants and to accept His will for your life?

Then listen to His voice; don't turn away from Him. Whatever you have done, whatever your lifestyle, makes no difference to Him, for as surely as He delivered Mary Magdalene, unquestionably He will do exactly the same for you!

You see, God wants you so much to experience intimately His great love through His Son Jesus Christ. Why don't you apply the *law of faith* to His calling and answer "yes?" I promise you, it will be a decision you will never regret, for as the Master calls, He also *always* keeps His word!

For God so loved the world that He gave his
only begotten Son, that whoever believes in Him
should not perish but have everlasting life.
(John 3: 16)

Chapter 2

A Prized Possession

Conversation ceased instantly. Where it once flowed easily, now no one dared say anything. Instead they watched, mesmerized, as Alicia silently entered the room. *How dare she interrupt their feast?*

Gathered in the room were no ordinary men. These were men of great influence; the elite of Jewish society. They were the Pharisees – the separated ones. They held the belief that God not only gave Moses a written law (the Torah) on Mount Sinai but also an oral law, which was open to *their* interpretation. The Pharisees kept themselves "pure" from defilement by strictly adhering to Levitical laws of purity with regard to rituals and moral principles. Naturally, they developed a self-righteous attitude to anyone who did not hold such beliefs or met with their expectations.

•

Behind Alicia came flustered servants, heads bowed and faces ashamed. "Master, we tried to stop her!"

Dollys Y Crooks

Shaun, the perfect, moral, upright Pharisee, whose home it was, simply stared, desperately trying to make sense of the scene before him. As he struggled to regain his composure, he silently screamed, *How dare she? She will surely pay for this!*

Having no confidence in his servants' ability to carry out the task of throwing her out, Shaun decided to do so himself. As he attempted to rise from the table, it was as though an unseen force held him down. He tried again and again but encountered the same result. He could only sit and glare angrily at the woman who had dared to cross the threshold of his house, especially a woman of her type.

He watched in horror as Alicia headed straight for his distinguished guest seated at his right hand. It was easy to spot his guest amongst the chosen ones. His garment was not as lavish and pompous as theirs. It was simple, yet something about Him separated Him from the others. It was not just His garments. There was such tenderness in His eyes, and His face shone with kindness.

His was the only face Alicia focused on, and as she drew closer, He seemed to communicate that He understood her desperation. In the midst of such a gathering, Shaun's guest truly stood out.

His kind gesture made Alicia weep, and each step she made towards Him caused the volume of her tears to increase. When at last she reached His side, her tears were relentless. She knelt before Him and with those same tears washed His feet. Then, with gentle strokes, she dried them with her hair.

Next, she opened her alabaster jar of expensive perfume and poured it lavishly upon Him. Then she massaged its powerful scent into His feet, kissing each in turn. Oblivious

A Prized Possession

to everything and everyone around her, her work took on a rhythm all of its own – massage … kiss … massage … kiss.

Meanwhile, Shaun's distinguished guest sat, keenly aware of the feelings and thoughts of those around Him and smiled in amusement.

•

Where had she got such expensive perfume? Shaun forgot that his original intent was to throw her out himself, and his thoughts now turned to his distinguished guest. *What kind of a prophet is He, allowing a woman of her class to touch Him? A true prophet of God would never allow the likes of her to touch Him. Obviously, He does not know she is an unclean woman, a woman of the night.*

Not only had she broken the social code of the day by entering a room full of men uninvited (why, even Queen Esther could not approach King Ahasuerus unless he had summoned her), but as a woman of the night, her very presence had made Shaun's home unclean. He would surely have to purify it after the night was over!

"Woman, your sins are forgiven you. Your faith has saved you. Go in peace."

The words of his guest startled Shaun. Her sins, forgiven? Impossible! They were far too many. How could this be? A bewildered Shaun could only sit and shake his head from side to side.

•

Outwardly, Alicia was very beautiful. Inwardly, she hated herself. Her beauty had always brought problems with

Dollys Y Crooks

both men and women. Women were always envious of her, and though she had dated the best of men, she was never quite sure whether they wanted her for herself or just as a trophy to add to their many accomplishments.

Her first husband, Kevin, had abused her physically. She was his "property," he often reminded her, and as such he could do whatever he wanted with and to her. He had died in a road accident three years ago, and Alicia had a hard time pretending to be the grieving widow. She, for one, was relieved he was dead.

Shortly after her husband's death, Alicia met another man and fell head over heels in love with him. His name was Patrick, and he promised her the earth. Her friends tried to warn her that something about Patrick wasn't quite right, though they couldn't put their finger on it. To her anxious friends, she would always reply, "I love him. Even if what you are saying is true, I can change him. You watch and see."

Alicia realized when it was too late – and when her feelings for him were too strong – that Patrick was a man who preyed on vulnerable women and had no desire to change his ways. He ran an escort agency with many women like her on his books – widowed, divorced, and vulnerable. At first, he would ask her to meet a "friend" of his. It soon became a regular routine, with the number of "friends" increasing all the time.

After a short while, Alicia found herself "escorting" for Patrick's gain. Sadly, the truth came home to her. You can't change anyone but yourself. Trapped in a lifestyle she hated, she reasoned, *At least I'm not being physically abused. Which one's worse, though?* There was no need for an answer because either way she was still someone else's property. What else

A Prized Possession

could she do? She had no skills as such to support herself, and she certainly would not rely on handouts. She was too proud for that.

Kevin had never wanted her to work. He insisted that he would be the provider, hence his philosophy that she was his property. Shame and embarrassment kept her from turning to her friends. Even if she wanted to, she couldn't; Patrick made sure of that. Feeling cut off from everyone she knew, Alicia slowly slipped into deep, dark despair.

•

Her looks assured she was always busy, and Patrick did his part by being very careful not to damage his precious commodity, especially as her clients were all distinguished, well-respected men. Most had families of their own whose wives just did not "understand" them.

To see Alicia from the outside, you would think she had it all, but as she climbed in bed during the early hours of the morning, she would simply cry herself to sleep. Her pain was not visible but hidden deep inside. All she had ever wanted was to marry a nice man, settle down, and have children. How she wished she had listened to her friends when they tried to protect her. Was love truly real, or was it only a figment of people's imagination?

•

On her way home one evening, just as she was about to cross into the street in which she lived, someone smiled and handed her a small slip of paper. Alicia took it, promptly screwed it up, and was about to toss it away when she heard

Dollys Y Crooks

a soft, still voice say, "Keep it. Read it when you get home." The word *creepy* sprang to mind. Shuddering, Alicia placed the slip of paper in her handbag and thought no more of it.

•

The next morning, she awoke to a brilliant ray of sunshine sweeping across her bed. Stretching her body as far as it could go Alicia sighed, "Will I ever live an ordinary life? Settle down and have children?"

Gently brushing away the teardrops from her cheeks, Alicia glanced upwards to the place where her treasure chest sat. There were so many memories in that chest, things she had treasured all her life, which was why she called it her treasure chest.

She climbed out of bed and headed to her prized chest. Then she slowly returned with it and unlocked it. Inside were a doll, a ring, a necklace, and a card, mementoes she had kept even from childhood. Then as her eyes settled on the last item in the chest, a warm glow filled her entire being. This was her most prized possession. She had saved for a long time to buy this alabaster jar filled with expensive perfume.

The doll was her favourite toy growing up. It was her constant companion as a little girl. Alicia laughed out loud, "If this doll could have talked, it would have revealed all my secrets to Mother."

The ring was her second piece of "real" jewellery. It was of pure gold, studded with diamonds, and complemented by an opal stone in its centre. It was the only item that held pleasant memories of her few good times with Kevin. The necklace had been a family heirloom for four generations.

A Prized Possession

It always went to the firstborn girl – but would she be able to pass it on to a fifth generation?

Her thoughts wandered upon her own family. She had not seen them since Kevin died. He was the apple of her mother's eye. If only she knew the truth about him. What if Mother knew the truth about Alicia's lifestyle? Vigorously, she shook her head. Time to move on.

She spent time reminiscing over the next item. It was a card Leah, her best friend, had given to her. They were in the same class at primary school, and their friendship continued into adulthood. One day Leah became ill and was found to have cancer. Alicia's whole world collapsed, but she determined in herself to be strong for her best friend. Many times she would ask the question, How could this happen to someone so kind and loving? She remembered how even then life had seemed unfair.

Pulling her mind from the past and into the present, Alicia glanced again at her alabaster jar. It contained a blend of the finest scents available, all blended together as one. Each time she opened the jar, its sensual smell transported her into another world –a world of love and romance. She would keep this for her wedding night, for the man who would love her just for herself. He would be the one worthy of this precious, priceless possession of hers.

All the other mementoes represented her past, but this insignificant item, as it might appear to some, represented her future. Gently resting the treasure chest on the floor, Alicia mused to herself, "A girl can dream can't she?" These were the last words she remembered saying as she smiled, wrapped her arms around herself, and fell into a deep sleep once again.

Dollys Y Crooks

•

A week passed, and Alicia forgot all about the note she had been given that night. Preparing to enter the shower, she glimpsed her handbag out of the corner of her eyes. She felt an urge to look inside, not knowing what she was looking for, and came across the slip. It read:

Revival Meeting, 23rd and 24th November
Are you lonely? Are you weary of life?
Seeking a better life?
Then this meeting is for you!
Come and hear the Man of God
as He ministers God's Word.
Whatever your needs are, He can meet them!
Don't hesitate, don't wait, it might be too late!

Can someone really do that? They can actually help me? They can change my life? Forgetting all about showering, Alicia headed straight for the kitchen and looked at the calendar. The 23rd and 24th – that was last week. Anxiously, she looked at the slip again and saw a telephone number at the bottom. With fingers trembling, she dialled the number.

Brr … brr … brr … No answer.

She tried again. Still no answer.

"No!" Alicia screamed down the telephone. "I need someone to talk to. I need someone to help me change my life. Please, someone, please answer the telephone."

Brr … brr … brr … "Pick up the telephone! Hold on girl, don't put it down. Hold on, let it ring just for a little while longer." Alicia sighed as she flopped to the floor. "It's

A Prized Possession

no use. Who am I kidding? My life will never change. Just for a moment, I was silly enough to believe that it could."

With defeatist thoughts rampaging through her mind, a disheartened Alicia was about to put the telephone down when she suddenly heard a breathless voice say, "Hello, can I help you?"

Alicia screamed, "Yes, you can!"

Out of her mouth came jumbled words that made no sense as she struggled to explain about the slip, the meeting, and the fact that she had missed the dates mentioned.

"You are not making sense," the lady replied. "Could you speak a bit slower, please?"

In response to the calm and reassuring voice of the lady, Alicia composed herself and explained her situation, as well as her disappointment.

"There really is nothing I can do for you," replied the voice on the end of the telephone. "The meetings are over, and the speaker is preparing to leave town. Tonight will be his last."

Sheer desperation drove Alicia to ask, "Where will he be spending it? Please tell me."

"I am sorry, that is confidential information," the lady replied.

"Please," Alicia begged.

Hearing the urgent plea in Alicia's voice, the woman relented. "He will be dining at the home of Shaun, the Pharisee. Please don't tell anyone I told you."

"I promise," Alicia said. "Thank you so very much."

Replacing the telephone on its receiver, Alicia declared, "Tonight, I *shall* change my life!"

Dollys Y Crooks

Then a sudden fear came upon her like a dark cloud covering a bright blue sky. How? Tonight was a working night. As suddenly as fear came, so too was the thought to pray. Pray, where did that come from? Alicia remembered her grandmother had taught her how to pray when she was a little girl, but it held no significance to her. It was just Grandma.

Alicia now slipped out of her robe and entered the shower. While the water streamed down her back, she prayed, "God, when I was small, my granny taught me to pray. She said it was a very important thing to do and that You like it when we pray. I would often kneel and pray to You, although it was only when I visited Granny. But as I grew up, You seemed so far away and so unreal. If You truly are real, God, please change me. I don't want to live like this anymore. I am tired, so tired. Please help me."

Alicia finished showering, still unsure what her next move should be. If God was real, did He hear her? *Furthermore, does He hear women like me?*

•

Excitement replaced the fear of Patrick, and Alicia sensed that the change she was about to encounter would lead her to experience the reality of God. A wonderful thought crossed her mind. She would dress as a seller, take her precious alabaster jar, and pretend she had come to show her wares to Shaun and his guests.

Everyone knew Shaun. He was an outstanding citizen in her town. In fact, he was so moral and upright that he would never allow the likes of her into his home. He would

A Prized Possession

simply say that her presence would make his home unclean. She belonged on the streets, not in his house.

Alicia did not dare stop to think of the repercussions that might follow her actions, for fear of aborting her plan. Why should she allow people's opinions to stop her from gaining a new life? She would bypass every one of them. This was about *who* she really was and *what* she wanted. It was about her life, her hopes, her dreams, and her ambitions, not *what* she was! People only saw her for *what* she was. No one ever took the time to discover *who* the real Alicia was.

At that moment, Patrick crossed her mind, and fear rose up in her heart again. *What will he do?* Reminding herself that she had prayed and later felt God had answered her prayers, Alicia concluded that surely God would protect her, just as her friends had once tried to.

"I don't care what it takes," said Alicia, finding the courage to carry on. "I can't miss this opportunity. This man may never return again."

•

What to wear? Alicia opened her wardrobe and tried on one garment after another, but they all seemed inappropriate. Then it dawned on her: she would have to disguise herself in order to get into Shaun's home. After all, the whole town knew who and what she was. She wouldn't stand a chance if she went as herself.

Excitedly, Alicia made her way to the mall in town, careful to avoid all the places she knew Patrick would be. At the first store, she bought a long black frilly skirt, ankle-high leather boots, a multicoloured sweater made of wool, and a long black scarf with pearls on its tassels. Seeing her

Dollys Y Crooks

reflection in the mirror, she thought of her grandmother and wondered how she was. Then Alicia headed quickly for the store's front entrance before she had a chance to change her mind.

•

Clutching her alabaster jar, Alicia made her way to Shaun's home. What would she do once inside? She would pray. "One step at a time," she reasoned. It didn't take long to reach Shaun's home. From where she was standing, she could see the lights and hear laughter coming from inside.

Heart thumping and fingers trembling, she knocked on Shaun's door with "what if?" thoughts bombarding her mind. Bravely she told herself, *Come on, girl, you can do this. Just remain focused. Keep the goal in sight.*

A servant answered the door, and she produced her expensive alabaster jar. "Please let the owner of the house know that I am here," she said confidently and politely.

"He is dining with his guests," came the reply.

"I know," Alicia boldly stated. "That's why I am here. He asked me to come and show my wares to his guests."

As the servant turned to inform her master, Alicia promptly followed her, taking no notice of the sumptuous surroundings of Shaun's home. Just before she reached the dining room where Shaun and his guests were seated, the scarf she had on her head slipped to her shoulders.

Before Alicia could retrieve it, another servant gasped, "What are *you* doing here? Who let you in?"

Too late. The first servant had already opened the door that led to the dining room, and as Alicia stood at its entrance with her scarf draped across her shoulders, every

28

A Prized Possession

eye was riveted upon her. Nothing and no one was going to take this moment from her. This was her night.

•

The silence was unbearable as she headed in the direction of Shaun's distinguished guest. Approaching Him, Alicia sensed something clean and soul-stirring about Him. His eyes were tender, and His face was kind. He seemed to understand her desperation. She felt His holiness, and the closer she got to Him, the more her lifestyle amplified.

Racked with guilt, she began to weep, her tears flowing uncontrollably. She had risked everything to enter this moral, upright man's home, yet as she stood in front of his distinguished guest, shame covered her in a way she had never known. She had gotten used to the name calling and the insults of both men and women, but there was something different about this man. She suddenly cared about what He thought and dared not look at Him face to face.

Perhaps there would be no need to tell Him who she was; hopefully, her actions would speak loudly for her. Slowly, kneeling before Him in repentance, Alicia bowed her head in reverential awe, her tears falling silently on His feet as she opened her alabaster jar.

In the presence of all those seated in the room, Shaun's distinguished guest gently lifted her face to His and wiped away a tear from her cheek. Then, with a voice filled with kindness and compassion, He spoke words of comfort, healing, and wholeness to her. It was now His turn to minister to her.

Dollys Y Crooks

•

At that moment, Alicia felt He knew of her fears, her life, and her potential to become more than what she was now. Though she had never met Him personally until now, she knew He understood her hurt, her pain, her disappointments, and her desperation to risk so much for a change of life. As He continued to minister to her, Alicia's heart, her soul, and her spirit felt washed and cleansed.

Two words He had spoken to her made an indelible impression. The first was *forgiven*. That was exactly how Alicia felt. Her slate had been wiped clean, and she'd been given a chance to start afresh. All along, He had been the missing piece in this puzzle she called her life.

His second word was *faith*. Did faith mean "sheer desperation?" For Alicia it was that, for she believed He was the only one able to change her life, and He did not disappoint her.

In her lifetime, she had received so little, yet this faith He had spoken of had given her incredibly much in a very short time. Alicia concluded she had much to learn about this thing He had called *faith*.

•

With renewed courage and a sense of wholeness, Alicia left her empty alabaster jar, her most prized possession, at His feet and bowed before Him for the last time. There would be no need to keep it now. She had found Him – One so worthy of its precious contents and One upon whom she had lovingly bestowed it.

A Prized Possession

Then, as silently as Alicia had entered, she left. If anyone had not actually witnessed it, they would never have believed it truly happened.

•

This story is found in Luke 7: 36–50.
The true characters are Jesus, Simon the Pharisee,
and a woman in the city.

•

Can you identify with the woman in this story? Do you think that what you are and where you are, you will always be? Do you think the life you are living now is hell on earth? Are you desperate enough to make a change?

Then I have news for you. Jesus is alive today as He was then. What He did for this woman, He will do for you. Surely, I hear you say, life can't be worse than this? Yes, it can! Eternity without Jesus is worse than any lifestyle you are currently living in.

Why don't you come to Him today, believe on Him, and accept His love for you? Only He can change your life permanently here on earth and give you eternal life when your earthly one expires. He's waiting. Don't leave it too long.

And you will seek Me and find Me,
when you search for Me with all your heart.
(Jeremiah 29: 13)

Chapter 3

When Life Just Doesn't Make Sense

Marsha felt she was born in church. She could not remember a day when she was not on her way to church, in church, or on her way home from church. Both her parents were pastors long before it was fashionable for women to preach the Word of God. Daddy had no problems in allowing Mum to fulfil her calling, for he knew that she supplied whatever he lacked, and vice versa.

Marsha wasn't really complaining; she actually loved church. She loved the company of the other children, as she was an only child. She loved the old ladies who always brought her gifts; she loved to play the piano and to listen to her mum and dad preach God's Word.

•

Marsha was a good girl who always obeyed her parents and was top of the class in many of her subjects at school. As she grew and saw the many mistakes girls her age made, she

When Life Just Doesn't Make Sense

thanked God over and over again that she had kept herself. You see, she did not flirt with the boys, she had never got pregnant, nor had she had an abortion.

In fact at twenty-two years old, Marsha could count on her fingers the number of dates she had been on. It wasn't that she was ugly or anything like that. It was just that Mum and Dad didn't think anyone was decent enough for their little girl. Some of the young women she sang with in the choir were happily married, but a few, like Lucinda, Annette, and Beatrice, were either separated or divorced or lived miserable married lives. Other young women had travelled the world, experiencing new places and cultures; still others had remained at home happy in what they were doing.

Sometimes, Marsha wondered whether she would ever get married or still be playing the piano at age sixty-four, unmarried. She laughed at such a thought. Surely God would not allow that to happen to her. Hadn't she been faithful to Him and the things concerning Him? Hadn't she faithfully adhered to the Scripture, "Children, obey your parents in the Lord, for this is right" (Ephesians 6: 1)? She had done this even through her teenage years, and now that she was an adult, nothing had changed. Hadn't she always paid her tithes and offerings as she was taught, even as a child? She could see no possible reason why God would ever withhold a good husband from her.

•

One Saturday, Daddy told her that the Rev. Andre Stewart was coming to preach at church. Daddy had tried several times to engage him, but his busy schedule hadn't

Dollys Y Crooks

allowed him to do so until now. "No big deal." Marsha shrugged. Daddy had invited lots of preachers over the years. Why would this one be any different? But Daddy had spoken well of him and of his love for God, and as he did so, Marsha felt a stirring within her which she tried to ignore. Whenever Daddy spoke so well of someone, you had to sit up and take note.

Curious, she began to build a picture of this Rev. Andre Stewart in her mind. It was the usual tall, dark, and handsome picture. The thought did cross her mind that she could be wrong. He could be the exact opposite. Of course, she found strength to push *that* thought away.

•

Sunday arrived, and Rev. Stewart came with it too. No disappointments there. Rev. Andre Stewart was everything she had imagined him to be and much more. He was single! – one small detail Daddy had forgotten to mention. Marsha thought about how great it was being the daughter of pastors, although it also had its downside, for you were expected to be perfect, well mannered, and polite even when you didn't feel like it. Sometimes she couldn't wait to get home, kick off her shoes, and just be herself again. On the other hand, the places she visited and the people she met from various cultures and languages afforded Marsha priceless experiences. Some incidents she remembered fondly, others with embarrassment.

There was the time Mother invited a Turkish preacher home for dinner. After eating, a loud sounding belch could be heard from the visitor's direction. Mother's face went a strawberry red. Daddy first coughed and then smiled at

When Life Just Doesn't Make Sense

their guest. Marsha simply excused herself from the table, slowly walked out of the room, then ran to her bedroom and laughed until her sides ached. You would have done the same too, if you knew how prim and proper Mother was.

It was some time later they discovered that in the preacher's culture, belching after a meal was considered good table manners. It was a way of informing your host that the meal was delightful. When Marsha heard that, she laughed again. A simple "thank you" would have been sufficient, she thought to herself, especially in her mother's case.

•

Straying in the midst of the young preacher's sermon, Marsha wondered if anything strange or funny would happen. Then she pulled her mind back on track and began to listen intently. *Mmm, his preaching isn't that bad either,* she said to herself.

Rev. Stewart's sermon was taken from the Old Testament book of Job. He preached on how blessed a man is when he meditates and walks in obedience to the Word of God, expounding on the fact that God is able to protect His own. He taught the congregation that when the enemy seeks to bring destruction or pain into such a person's life, he can only do so when God grants him permission.

Rev. Stewart emphasized that God built hedges around such a person and all that pertained to him. Then, speaking words of comfort and hope, he encouraged the congregation that whatever situation or circumstance they were currently experiencing, God knew all about it and was able to turn it around for their good.

Dollys Y Crooks

"Hang on!" he said, punching his fist into the air. "Don't give up. God is counting on you, just like He did with Job. You will triumph!"

Marsha could testify to those words of his, for God had truly built a hedge around her life.

•

After church, dinner at their home went well. Mother used her best China ware and served her favourite meal – roast chicken, roast potatoes, parsnips, carrots, salad, and her special homemade coleslaw. Daddy always joked that if the brook ever dried up, they could sell Mother's coleslaw recipe for a living.

There were no hiccups or amusing stories to tell concerning Rev. Stewart. He was an excellent guest. Marsha found herself listening intently to his every word. Close up, he was much more handsome than she had thought this morning when she first saw him. Perhaps it was the rays of sunlight now shining through the window upon his face that made the difference. Whatever it was, Marsha found herself drawn to this young preacher who, she discovered in passing conversation, was only three years older than herself. His sound preaching and knowledge of God's word made him seem more mature than he actually was.

Marsha, however, was not the only one drawn to him. Mum and Dad were too. "This sure was a good sign," said Marsha and wondered if parents still paid a dowry for their daughters and whether it would apply to her.

•

When Life Just Doesn't Make Sense

Sometime later, Marsha discovered that the feeling was mutual. Rev. Stewart had shown an interest in her and approached her parents with a view to taking her out to dinner one evening. When she heard that Daddy had given his approval, she almost swooned. Then pretending to have a dancing partner, she waltzed as she praised God. "I knew You wouldn't let me down, God. Thank You. Thank You. I love You, God."

•

The day for Marsha's dinner date with Rev. Stewart finally came. Whilst she waited for him to arrive, Daddy read her the *Rule Book*. "Yes. Okay. Daddy, I promise," Marsha heard herself say repeatedly. Inwardly, she was screaming, *Daddy, I am twenty-two years old! Many girls my age are married, and some even have babies.* Outwardly and knowing better, Marsha kept silent. Nothing was going to ruin this evening.

After what seemed like hours, Rev. Stewart finally turned up – on time, a good sign to her parents, and promising to bring her home at a certain hour. The two waved goodbye and left for their first evening alone together. Rev. Stewart took Marsha to the finest restaurant in town. A good thing she had listened to Mother when she was training her on how to sit and what fork to use first. "Thank God for mothers," whispered Marsha with a smile.

Andre was the first to begin their conversation. "Please call me Andre," he said.

At first, it sounded strange, sort of lacking in respect, but after saying it a few times, Marsha felt more at ease.

Dollys Y Crooks

The evening was a delight. She wished it would never end. They had so much in common. They both loved to read biographies of men and women who had dedicated their lives to God, some renowned and others less familiar. They both loved to travel and discovered that each had a passion for teaching children. He had taught Sunday school classes and had been in charge of the youth group of his church before he became an itinerant preacher. She'd been a Sunday school teacher from the age of fifteen and assisted at summer camp and vacation Bible school in the autumn. She greatly looked forward to these two events all year round, for they were times of drawing closer to children in her church and helping new ones make decisions to become followers of Christ.

Glancing at his watch, Andre brought their conversation to an abrupt end. "I promised your parents I would bring you home at a certain time. I must keep my word. Let's go."

Reluctantly, Marsha rose from the table as Andre politely pulled her chair out, paid the bill and led the way to the restaurant's door, which he opened, allowing her to go first.

•

Mum and Dad pretended to be very busy as they heard Rev. Stewart's car approach the driveway to their home (in truth, they were peeking through the curtains every now and then). When the doorbell chimed, Daddy deliberately took his time to answer it. Unlocking the door slowly, he was met with a wide grin and sparkling eyes.

"Hi, Daddy, where's Mu …?"

When Life Just Doesn't Make Sense

Before Marsha could complete her sentence, her mother's head popped up from under Daddy's arm. "Here I am."

All three laughed. Turning towards Andre, Marsha extended her hands and said, "Thank you for a wonderful evening, Andre."

"The pleasure was all mine," he replied, returning her smile.

Shaking her parents' hands and wishing them a pleasant evening, Andre did an about turn and headed back to his car. Daddy closed the door after him and teased, "What's this 'Andre'? Whatever happened to 'Rev. Stewart'?"

All three laughed again, only this time loudly. Daddy kissed the cheek of his only child and headed for bed, leaving Mother and Marsha to sit up well into the night, of that he was sure.

·

Not long after, the couple announced their intention to be married and with the blessings of her parents and Andre's father, the wedding date was set. Not only had God rewarded Marsha's life of faithfulness by giving her a good husband; He had also rewarded her by giving her an anointed, rich husband. Andre's father was the owner of four farms and much livestock, as Marsha had later discovered.

After the wedding, Marsha attended Andre's church, Bethel Tabernacle, but was always careful to visit Daddy's church at least once a month. Solid Rock had been her whole life, and Andre did not expect her to sever ties entirely. Thank God, the distance was not too vast. Each day she kept in touch with Mother by telephone. Even so, it took some time for her to settle in at Bethel Tabernacle,

Dollys Y Crooks

particularly in regard to their way of worship. It was quite robust, while Solid Rock was quiet in its worship. Now, after three months, she was beginning to feel comfortable. She reasoned that, with Andre by her side, she could cope with anything.

•

One year into their marriage, Andre's father, Garfield, died suddenly. He had woken up one morning with chest pains. As they rushed him to hospital via the emergency services, he died en route.

His father's death was a bitter blow to Andre, for they shared a very close and special bond. Their relationship was not only that of father and son but also friends. Ever since the death of Andre's mother, Garfield had been his role model and mentor. His passing now left a huge gap in Andre's life. Marsha, reflecting on her own relationship with her parents, tried her very best to console him.

Garfield's death had also left Andre in a predicament. What road should he take? Should he sell the four farms his father owned, or would he be able to run them efficiently as well as perform his ministerial duties? There was no doubt in Andre's mind that he was called to preach the gospel of Jesus Christ, and further, he would never turn his back on this calling. Yet, out of respect, he owed it to his father to continue his life's work. Daily, Andre sought God for guidance.

•

When Life Just Doesn't Make Sense

As time went on, Andre felt the peace of God to continue both overseeing his father's farms and preaching the gospel. He employed men and women with the knowledge and relevant skills to run the farms from day to day, while he concentrated on preaching.

In time, Andre became a shrewd businessman, never making decisions on his own but always consulting God first. Through obedience to God's word, Andre prospered. In just a short time, he increased his late father's farms to seven, affording much needed employment to many people.

Marsha would often look at Andre, recall the first message she had heard him preach that Sunday at her father's church, and smile contentedly. God did indeed bless the man that meditated and walked in obedience to His Word. Life was so good that sometimes Marsha pinched herself to make sure she wasn't dreaming. Her husband loved her, and she loved him. Sometimes she felt that many envied Andre and wished at least one bad thing would happen to him. Regardless of her feelings, however, Andre continued to prosper.

•

Now confident as a businessman, Andre moved into the area of stocks and shares. Again, he prospered. It seemed to Marsha that her husband succeeded in everything he put his hand to. But Andre was not the only one to prosper.

Over the years, she gave birth to several sons and daughters. Their marriage was a partnership. She took care of the family while he took care of their needs. Marsha loved having children. She cherished her role as a wife and a mother. Taking care of her husband, their children, and the

Dollys Y Crooks

home was to Marsha her calling in life. It was her ministry. She had read what Proverbs 31 had said concerning the "virtuous woman" and particularly prided herself on verse 11: "The heart of her husband safely trusts in her …."

•

One weekend, while sitting outside on the back porch of their home, having breakfast, as was the couple's usual custom, Marsha looked over at her husband as he ate. She smiled as she thought of how he was still the same warm, kind, fascinating man she had met and married all those years ago. Though he'd gone a bit gray around the temples now, riches and success had not changed him, for he had kept close to the Giver of all things.

The only worry he seemed to have, every now and then, was the children. He worried that one of them might have sinned against God. Though they gave no cause for concern, being good, well-disciplined children (though none of them were angels), Andre still worried and would often give, aside from his usual tithes and offerings, huge donations on their behalf. It was at such times that Marsha would remind him of the first message he had preached at her father's church and ask, "Would God not also build a hedge around our children too?"

•

One hot summer's morning, the children were all camping out at their eldest brother's home, and Andre had left to go to the office, as some farm business needed sorting out. To all intents and purposes, it seemed like a normal

When Life Just Doesn't Make Sense

day. There were no bad dreams, no premonitions, nothing unusual. Stretching herself in bed, Marsha threw the covers aside, turned over to the nearby cabinet, and picked up a book she had been wanting to read for a long time. After reading a few chapters, Marsha eventually rose and was eating the delicious late breakfast her maid had prepared when the telephone rang.

"Miss, it's for you," the maid said.

"Hello," Marsha said. The voice on the other end was so incoherent that she had a hard time understanding it. "Hello," she tried again.

"Honey, all our shares have crashed. The security vans transporting the gold bars have been ambushed! One of the guards has been fatally wounded!"

Now recognizing his voice and trying to remain as calm as possible, Marsha replied, "Andre, Andre – what are you saying?"

In a barely audible voice Marsha heard, "Honey, I'm coming home. I can't take any more bad news. Not today."

Before she could say anything further, Andre hung up. In all the years they had been married, she had never heard him speak that way. Stunned by his call and losing all appetite for the delicious breakfast before her, Marsha sat down and looked around at her surroundings. What would happen to them now? Some of the children were still at private schools.

Distraught, she decided to climb back into bed, pull the covers over her head, and await Andre's entrance. He would pray and find a way; he always did.

A short while before Andre arrived home, the maid knocked incessantly on the couple's bedroom door. "What is it?" Marsha asked irritatingly.

Dollys Y Crooks

"Miss, Mr. Edward, the manager at Westfield Farm, is here to see you."

"Is it that urgent that you have to bang on my door like that?"

With head bowed and eyes lowered the maid replied, "I am afraid so, Miss."

Slowly, Marsha followed the maid; her mind refusing to accept that more bad news was on the horizon.

Standing in the hallway was Mr. Edward with his clothes torn and face blackened. In shock, Marsha asked, "What happened to you, Mr. Edward? What's going on?"

"There was an explosion on the farm and all the workers are dead. I alone managed to escape to bring the news to you."

Grasping for a chair to steady her nerves, Marsha sat down. Yesterday there was such calm. Life was peaceful. Everything was tranquil and serene. But today was a nightmare. She felt as if all the forces of hell had been unleashed upon them.

Andre entered the house just in time to receive the news Mr. Edward had brought. His eyes searched Marsha's for answers to many questions. Having no answers, Marsha stretched out her arms and walked over to her husband. The only thing she managed to say was, "Honey, I am sorry. I am so sorry." Reaching for her, Andre held his wife safely in his embrace as Mr. Edward silently left the hallway and made his way out the front door. He was sure that tomorrow Mr. Stewart would put everything in order.

But no sooner had Mr. Edward left than in came Michael, who watched over the couple's children. With

When Life Just Doesn't Make Sense

tears in his eyes and head bowed, he gave them even more devastating news than Mr. Edward.

"All your children were having lunch at their eldest brother's home," Michael paused, choked with emotion and desperately trying to pace his words, "when without warning, an earthquake hit the town. All your children are dead."

Marsha screamed hysterically and pounded her fists into Andre's chest. In all the years singing on the church choir, she never knew she could reach such a high pitch.

"What's going on, Andre? What's happening?" she asked.

Andre held his wife's clenched fists with all the strength he could muster. He had no answers to either his wife's questions or his own. Untangling herself from his grasp, Marsha slumped to the floor and began to rock herself back and forth, all the time muttering, "No. Not my babies. Not my babies."

After a while she felt no emotion and became unaware that those words were still coming from her lips.

•

Sometime later, she came to herself again, and her eyes searched for her Andre. He had moved as she had untangled herself from his grasp. Where was he? Where did he go? Was he rocking too? Seeing him and knowing he was close by would make everything okay again. Though there were no words either of them could say to comfort the other, Marsha knew she would feel safe once more if she could just see him. Right now, a numbness overshadowed her that she

Dollys Y Crooks

was incapable of describing. Where was he? Where was her rock? Where was her man?

Then her eyes found him. First he knelt in prayer, and then he prostrated himself on the marble floor, worshipping God. Marsha forgot all about wanting to be near him and feel his safe arms around her.

How could he worship God at a time like this? Seeing Andre lying there, words he had spoken in yesterday's meditation came flooding back to her.

"Honey, always worship God," he had said. "It is because of Him that we have all we have."

Marsha had to admit she had allowed her prayer life and Bible reading to become a bit sporadic. She was far too busy with the house and the children. Hadn't God given her a husband, a priest over her household, who made sure daily family meditations were carried out? Andre was the head of their home; she was the submissive wife, contented and happy in his love and experience of God. Andre could touch God's throne at any time. There was no need for her to do so while he was around.

As Marsha continued to watch her husband, prostrate on the floor and weeping before God, totally oblivious to anything and anyone else around him, anger rose up in her. How could God do this to them? Hadn't she been faithful to Him all her life? Didn't Andre always try his best to listen and obey Him? Would they ever be able to rebuild their lives again? All her children were dead, and what was a home without children? What would they do now? What would Andre do?

Weak and distraught, Marsha rose up from the floor and headed straight for bed. No sense in crying now. What

When Life Just Doesn't Make Sense

good would it accomplish? Would tears bring her children back? How she wished she could turn the clock back. Today would be yesterday, and tomorrow would never come.

•

In the days that followed, Andre continued to carry out his ministerial duties. The church tried several times to lighten them for him, but he insisted that he needed to continue. He could not and would not stop.

Andre also tried to put things in order concerning the business. He visited Mr. Johnson and Michael. He visited the families of his dead workers, assuring them they would be taken care of. He assisted the police with their investigation into the missing gold bars and met with his advisors concerning the shares and the future of Westfield Farm.

As for the loss of his children, Andre felt lost and inadequate. Marsha was on the brink of a nervous breakdown, and though he tried many times to console her, she only sank deeper into despair. The women of the church were great, and many rallied around her to offer help and support. Marsha, however, in her state of mind, felt they came to gloat over her tragedy and refused help from them all. She asked Andre not to allow any of them into their home. How Andre wished her parents, who had died a few years ago in a plane crash, were still alive. They would know what to do. They would know how to bring their daughter out of the dreadful place she was currently in.

Reminders of their children's absence were all around, and Andre could not bear the thought of losing his wife too. He had to be strong, as strong as he'd ever been. He

Dollys Y Crooks

knew it would be an impossible task on his own and that the only way to be successful would be to keep close to his God. Though he did not understand why years of serving Him had brought them to this end, he knew, in his heart, that this was not really the end.

The God he served and preached about would never allow him to end a life of faithful testimony to His goodness, His protection, and His blessings in such a manner. No, there had to be an answer for all this, but what?

In time, Andre reasoned, his God would reveal why He'd given the enemy permission to bring such devastating destruction into their lives. For now, he was sure of this one thing, God was counting on him not to give up. Knowing this gave Andre the motivation he so desperately needed to continue, for he just could not let his God down.

•

The sad day came to bury their children, and Marsha lay in bed all day. This day did not exist for her. *Let Andre do it; he's the strong one.* She would remember *life* today, not death. She would keep the happy memories of her children, their laughter and their tears, even their squabbles. Her heart was too broken to be pieced together again, and she had grown bitter towards the God she had served all her life. Just because she had let slip her prayer life and Bible reading was no reason to take her children from her. *And Andre – faithful, strong Andre – what did he do?*

•

When Life Just Doesn't Make Sense

Andre continued to be strong for his wife, while still clinging to his God. The decision was made not to rebuild Westfield Farm. He invested in new stocks, and though the gold bars were never recovered, slowly finances began to improve. Marsha too began to make progress, but just when it looked like she would make a full recovery, tragedy struck again. This time it was Andre. She had noticed he was not eating very well, which was quite unusual for him. Whenever she asked him if anything was wrong, he always replied, "I'm just not hungry, that's all."

But as he grew thinner and thinner, boils began to appear on his skin. Marsha begged him to see Dr. Walker. One day, without her knowledge, Andre went.

Shocked at his condition, Dr. Walker immediately ran various tests and asked him to return. He had been their doctor since the birth of their fourth child, and they had developed a friendship. Dr. Walker had been a tremendous support to Andre and Marsha when their children died and also through Marsha's depression. Now, here Andre was seeking his help and advice once again.

Returning to Dr. Walker's office a week later and not knowing what to expect, Andre listened as his doctor and friend explained that his condition was unlike any he had known in twenty-five years of practising medicine. He had contacted a few of his colleagues, and they were all baffled. There was no treatment he could prescribe for Andre's condition; he could only keep a constant check on him.

Shaking his head sadly, Dr. Walker said, "Andre, I am so sorry. The only thing that can help you now is a miracle. How is Marsha taking it?"

Blushing, Andre told him she was unaware of his visit.

Dollys Y Crooks

"Would you like me to speak to her?" Dr. Walker enquired.

"She is just coming out of her depression. I don't want to make things worse."

"But Andre, she has to know," Dr. Walker replied gently.

"All right," whispered Andre.

"That's settled, tomorrow at noon then."

Smiling faintly, Andre left Dr. Walker's office in a daze. Looking up to the sky, he asked, "Lord, are You there? What's going on? I am not sure I can take any more. What did I do wrong? Was there something I should have done or didn't do? You know my heart; search it and tell me, please. I know You are my Redeemer and that one day I shall see You face to face. Is that day soon?" Bitter tears trickled down Andre's cheeks as he made his way home.

•

Marsha was sitting on the back porch enjoying the sunshine upon the beautiful scenery that was their back garden. Upon hearing her husband's footsteps, she looked up.

"Hi, honey. Where have you been?" she asked.

"Oh, just for a walk," he replied.

"That was a long walk. Where did you end up?"

Andre, unable to pretend any longer, sat down beside her and took her hands. "I went to see Dr. Walker today."

"You did?" she asked excitedly. "I knew you would. What did he say? Did he give you a prescription to clear up these boils and bring back your appetite?"

Cupping the sides of his wife's face, Andre tenderly replied, "No, honey. He doesn't know what is wrong with me. He is coming tomorrow at noon to speak with you."

When Life Just Doesn't Make Sense

Placing her hands over his, Marsha shook her head slowly and murmured, "Andre, I can't take any more."

Gently, she removed his hands from her face, rose from her chair, and began pacing the floor of the porch, stopping only once to look at her husband. Covered in boils, Andre looked like an aged man rather than one in his early fifties.

Seeing her stop to look at him, Marsha's once strong husband, her rock, her place of safety, rose and hobbled towards her. Struggling to control her anger and losing the battle, Marsha screamed, "Andre, curse God and die! There is nothing left for us. Just curse Him. If you won't, I will!" Nothing made sense to her anymore. She had countless *why* questions to which she had no answers.

Andre looked at his wife through eyes filled with pain. Then he opened his mouth and, with a determination that did not match his physical condition, tenderly replied, "Marsha, you speak as a foolish woman. If we can receive so much good at the hand of God, then we must be able to accept when things go wrong also."

"Andre!" she screamed between sobs. "I have lost my children. He took all of them. They are gone, Andre, gone, and now He wants to take you!"

"No, Marsha. I am still here," he whispered. "We still have each other."

"But for how long? There is no cure for your sickness. You said yourself that Dr. Walker doesn't even know what it is. I can't live without you by my side, Andre. If you go, I will too."

Holding Marsha's hand and walking with much difficulty, Andre led his wife back to her chair. "Hush, Marsha," he said gently, as he sat down beside her. "Perhaps

Dollys Y Crooks

this is a test to see whether our trust is in all He has given us or in Him personally. I know you haven't spent much time with Him for a while. I thought I could cover you with my prayers. Come, honey, let's pray."

Marsha slipped to her knees humbly and submissively before her husband, her prince, and her friend. Placing her head in Andre's lap, she wept non-stop. Her tears were like torrents of rain. Every pain, every pent-up frustration, and all her grief and anger at losing her children came gushing out.

She told God how much she had hated Him and asked for His forgiveness. She asked Him for help to be strong during Andre's illness. She promised Him that she would spend more time praying and reading her Bible the way she used to.

Andre laid his hand on his wife's head and asked his God to forgive the foolish words she had spoken in anger and to bless her. He told God how much he loved her and needed her by his side. He prayed for himself and asked for strength too to face whatever lay ahead for both of them. Then as dusk began to settle in, Andre ended his prayer with, "Amen. Your will be done, Lord."

"Yes, Lord," Marsha replied in agreement. Her heart was at peace both with her God and herself.

As she looked up at Andre's face, he noticed a softness in her face and a glow in her eyes he had not seen for quite some time. They knew that whatever happened now, they would continue to handle it together, as they had always done.

Marsha could now face those painful memories and was confident that whatever the future held for them, whether

When Life Just Doesn't Make Sense

good or evil, they were in God's hands. Again she was assured that His hands was always the best place to be in.

•

Andre's healing did come. Marsha bore other children, and the business prospered more than Andre could ever have imagined. His God proved to one and all that He was not just the provider of blessings and abundance but that He was also the Healer and the Miracle Worker—in fact, He is the "I AM," whatever you need Him to be.

Marsha remembered that first message her husband had preached at her father's church, so very long ago, and could testify for herself now that his God, her parents' God, and now her God did indeed protect, bless and build hedges around those who served Him. She could also affirm by personal experience now that even when He gave permission for the hedge to be removed and you suffered great adversity, it was only because He had boasted of you. Once you passed the test through *faith*, He would give you much more than you had in the first place.

Through these painful experiences, Marsha came to realize that though she had been in church all her life, sung in the church choir, obeyed her parents, and done all that was required of her, she had never known God intimately. As a child and young person, she had lived on her parents' experience of Him. Then later, when she became a married woman, she lived on her husband's experience. From now on, she would live on her own experience and enjoy all it had to offer.

•

Dollys Y Crooks

This story is found in Job, chapters 1, 2, and 42.
The true characters are God, Job and his wife.

•

Is all hell let loose in your life, your home, or your job? Do you feel like you just can't take any more? Do you have an intimate relationship with God? Then perhaps He is boasting of you!

It may not feel like it right now, but it is the truth. He is asking this question to your enemy and mine, "Have you considered my servant …?" {*Insert your name here*}. There is no need to be afraid, because God is the One who is doing the boasting.

There was a point in Job's life when he just could not take any more. It was then that God stepped in and strengthened him. He won't give you more than you are able to handle. If you continue to trust Him, He will do the same for you as He did for Job.

Remember, it is God that is doing the boasting. And when the test is over, He will give you much more than you had in the first place. He has it all under control – His control! Continually put *the law of faith* into action, and watch Him.

For I know the thoughts that I think toward
you, says the LORD, thoughts of peace and not
of evil, to give you a future and a hope.
(Jeremiah 29: 11)

Chapter 4

Nightmares Tell a Story

These nightmares! Each night was the same – the same dream, the same scene. Jaycinth would be awakened by a scream only to find Chante, tossing, turning, and crying. She had convinced herself that her daughter was only having bad dreams. Though she had found the blood-stained sheets hidden in the child's closet, she refused to accept her version of what had happened to her. *Things like this just don't occur in* my *kind of family,* she reasoned.

Chante was Jaycinth's only child, while she was her father's fourth child, due to his previous marriage.

•

Friday was always washday in Jaycinth's household. As she went to change the sheets on Chante's bed, she realized they were not the same set she had put on the previous Friday. Thinking that perhaps the child had wet the bed (as she had done on previous occasions), Jaycinth paid no great attention to the changed sheets and proceeded to strip

Dollys Y Crooks

the bed. It was then that she discovered bloodstains on the child's mattress.

How strange, she said to herself. *Chante is far too young to be menstruating.* Then she searched for the missing sheets and found them in the child's closet.

Gently, she called Chante and asked what happened. Faced with the blood-stained sheets, Chante broke down. Sobbing her little heart out, she told her mother what had happened that day when she left her alone with Daddy.

"Mummy, he told me it was our secret – that I must never tell you, or else he would have to go far, far away and we would never see him again. He said that he would buy me that new bicycle with all the latest gadgets I had been asking for, but *only* if I kept quiet." Waves of relief swept over the child. At last, she'd been able to tell someone and unburden herself.

Shocked, Jaycinth felt the room spinning out of control. Grasping for the head of Chante's bed, she quickly sat down before her feet had a chance to give way under the weight of her body. She had wondered why Errol suddenly became eager to purchase the bicycle when he had previously opposed it and why Chante did not make a fuss when earlier she had wanted it so badly.

This couldn't be happening in *her* family. She had heard about such events and read about them in the newspapers. She even knew some people everyone thought it was happening to, but it could *never* happen in *her* family. They were middle class, intellectual people, not like that Jones woman down the road, who had no husband and a different father for every one of her six children. No, Jaycinth's family was decent and respectable.

Nightmares Tell a Story

Calmly, she took the crumpled sheets from the floor. She would wash them so clean that no stain would ever remain on them. Turning to her daughter, Jaycinth said, "Chante, no-one must ever know. Your father must never know you told me. Do you hear me?"

The child simply nodded. Jaycinth knelt down by the side of the bed and began to scrub the mattress frantically, hoping to eradicate every trace of the child's blood and to erase its sight from her memory. She knew Chante had been acting strange this past week but had waited for her to explain why. This was one of Chante's quirks. She was not a talkative child. She had moments when she would come out of her shell and talk, after which she would become silent again for a long time afterwards. It was such a moment Jaycinth had been waiting for.

•

From that day on, Jaycinth lived a life of numbness, denial, and every now and then, when she couldn't avoid memories of the event, guilt. What was she to do? Take Chante and leave him? The truth would then come out, and the family would be broken up. No, she would continue to live with him as his wife, for the sake of her family.

•

That fatal day, Jaycinth had left Chante alone with her father Errol to go shopping. Nothing was unusual in that; she had often done so. After all, he was her dad, and she had no reason to suspect foul play.

Dollys Y Crooks

Chante had just emerged from the shower with a towel wrapped around her small body when she noticed her dad leaning against the wall in the corridor across from the bathroom door. He looked at her in a way that made her feel very uneasy.

"Hi, Daddy," she called out as she passed him on the way to her bedroom.

For the first time in her life, Chante felt afraid of her dad and wished that Jaycinth might return home at that very instant. Safe in her room and about to remove her towel to lotion her skin, Chante sensed something evil was about to happen. Instinctively, she reached for the lock on the door, but before she could get there, the knob turned, and the door opened. Daddy stood in front of her with that same look in his eyes.

Paralyzed with fright, the young child stood still, her towel bundled at her feet. After Errol had finished violating his daughter, she headed for the bathroom once more and stayed there until Jaycinth returned.

•

Jaycinth arrived home as Errol sat watching the sports channel.

What's new? she said to herself. "Hi, honey," she said cheerily. "Where's Chante?"

"I think she's upstairs," Errol said nonchalantly.

After unpacking the groceries, Jaycinth headed upstairs to show Chante what she had bought her. "Chante! Chante!" she called.

There was no answer. Jaycinth searched her room, "Chante! Chante!"

Nightmares Tell a Story

"In here," came a feeble voice.

"What's wrong, sugar? Aren't you feeling well?" Jaycinth asked as she knocked on the bathroom door.

"I'm okay, Mum. I'll be out in a minute," said Chante feeling safe now she knew her mum had returned home.

"Wait till you see what I bought you," her mother replied.

Chante tried her best to act normal, but Jaycinth sensed something was wrong. Knowing Chante, she asked once more but then decided to leave the matter alone. When Chante was ready, she would tell her.

•

In the days that followed, Chante became eerily quiet, sullen, and withdrawn. Jaycinth asked Errol if he knew what was wrong with her. Had she confided in him?

"No," he replied. "She's growing up. Maybe her hormones are kicking in."

The few times Chante had tried to confide in her mother, Errol somehow always appeared at that precise moment. Feeling his eyes piercing into hers, she would quietly excuse herself, go to her room, and sob. Ever since that fatal day, Chante always made excuses for not wanting to be alone with her father again, and even when others were around, she still remained far away from him.

•

It was during this time that Chante's nightmares began. She would awake at night screaming, "Go away. Leave me alone!"

59

Dollys Y Crooks

Each time, Jaycinth would rush to her daughter's bedside, hushing and embracing her until she drifted back to sleep. Many times Chante cried herself to sleep asking why. Why did her daddy do this to her? What did she do wrong? Sometimes, she even blamed herself. Was it somehow her fault? This was a heavy burden for a young girl to carry. Her daddy was meant to protect her, not hurt her, especially the way he had.

With Chante refusing to confide in her, Jaycinth made an appointment to see her class teacher to discuss if anything had happened at school. The answer was in the negative. She decided, once again, that when Chante was ready, she would open up to her.

It was only when she found the crumpled bed sheet in the cupboard that Jaycinth learnt the truth.

•

The child began to menstruate much earlier than her peers and as she entered her teenage years, she became very promiscuous and rebellious. Errol did nothing to control her, for fear she would expose him. Jaycinth did nothing to curb her rebellion, for fear her family would fall apart. For her part, Chante spoke to her father only when it was absolutely necessary.

•

As Chante grew into young adulthood, sex became like a drug. When her father had violated her, he opened doors for spirits of promiscuity, lust, and rebellion to enter her young life and take control. Together, they took up

Nightmares Tell a Story

residence in her and were so effective that the real Chante was no longer visible. She had grown from a lovely, shy girl to one who was barely recognizable. At fifteen years old, she became pregnant and her mother hurriedly arranged an abortion. For Jaycinth, life must go on. A year later, Chante became pregnant again. Jaycinth's solution was another secret abortion.

During the whole time, Chante's nightmares continued. After the second abortion Jaycinth tried to reason with her but only succeeded in arousing her anger.

"Two abortions – what's the big deal? The man who should have protected me, loved me, and nurtured me, violated me instead, and *you* kept quiet about it! I hate him, and I hate you!"

•

Now she was grown up, the thought of getting a proper job and training for a profession often crossed Chante's mind. Today, however, the thought remained constant. Looking at herself in the mirror, Chante asked, "What skills do I have? What am I good at?" Grinning slyly, with hands on her hips, she replied, "What am I good for is a more appropriate question."

It didn't take Chante long to figure out she was good at sex. "I know, I could open a brothel. I shall give it a more respectable name though, like the 'House of Chante.' Mum and Dad would cringe in horror!" She could just see their faces. Respectable, intellectual, middle-class family – hah!

"It's a secret, Chante. No one should ever know that this happened, Chante. I'll buy you that brand-new bike you've been asking for, Chante, with all the gadgets." Come to

Dollys Y Crooks

think of it, she never did ride that stupid new bike. "This will teach them!" Chante snarled as she sat down to formulate her plans.

•

True to form, once her business was up and running, Mum and Dad disowned her completely. Not even the thought of her spilling the beans kept them from doing so. They reasoned that it happened long ago, and no one would believe her now.

Chante's nightmares continued, but strangely, they weren't quite as intense now that she had launched the House of Chante.

Her strategy was a brilliant one. Customers were never scarce. The House of Chante employed ten girls and was located in a prime spot right after the toll gates at the entrance to the high street. It was a place where weary travellers who came from far away went seeking some fun away from home as well as those whose wives just "didn't understand them".

•

One thunderous, stormy late afternoon two strangers sought shelter at the House of Chante. They were not like the usual travellers. Something about them was different. Chante wondered whether these were the men who were currently making newspaper headlines, branded as dangerous because they always left a trail of destruction everywhere they went. These men were not to be entertained

Nightmares Tell a Story

at any cost. Roadblocks had been set up, troops placed on emergency alert, and a reward offered if they were sighted.

"How typical of the media, always stirring up people's emotions," sighed Chante.

Yet there was something unusual about these two men. If they were who the newspapers said they were, what were they doing in the House of Chante, and how did they get past the roadblocks? Curiosity welled up inside Chante. She had to find out for herself whether these were indeed the men she had read and heard about. Were they really as violent and dangerous as the media made them out to be? They certainly didn't look so. But if they were, perhaps she might be safer on their side rather than against them.

•

Cautiously, Chante took the men to a private room, invited them to sit down and brought food and drinks before them. Excited and nervous at the same time, she somehow forgot to offer them her usual hospitality. Suddenly, there came a sharp, incessant knock on the front door. Both men bolted upright. Chante could see the fear in their eyes as they looked at each other, wondering what their next move should be.

"Don't worry," Chante said calmly, "follow me."

Leading them out the back door, she quickly took them upstairs and hid both men in the loft. Then she straightened herself and, in her usual manner, opened the door to her establishment. Chante found herself face to face with three policemen. She apologized for the delay and asked demurely, "Yes, can I help you?"

Dollys Y Crooks

The men looked at her fondly. Officer Eugene smiled, remembering past times. Then he cleared his throat and replied, "Ah, Madam, we heard two strangers entered your place a short while ago, and we have come to investigate."

"Oh, yes. You are perfectly correct, Officer Eugene. Two men did enter the House of Chante today requiring refreshments, but as night was beginning to fall, they refused boarding and left. They said they were on a mission, had urgent business to attend to, and could not stop to enjoy my usual hospitality." She went on, maintaining eye contact with Officer Eugene, "They were heading to the mountains in the east. If you hurry, maybe you might catch them."

"Thank you, Madam," Officer Eugene responded, removing his helmet and bowing his head. "Please, be very careful. They are dangerous men and should not be entertained at any costs, whether by yourself or your girls. Goodnight."

The officers had no reason to doubt Chante. She had helped them many times with past enquiries, and they had always known her to be honest. She watched as the three officers left, heading in an easterly direction, and then quietly shut the door.

Later, once the day's transactions were completed with clients, she paid the girls and gave them the rest of the evening off. Looking at her in disbelief, they speedily gathered their belongings and left promptly, just in case she changed her mind. For Chante, the men upstairs were more important now.

•

Nightmares Tell a Story

Eagerly, Chante ran upstairs to the loft where the hidden men were. They knew she would be expecting answers from them, and because she had saved their lives, they felt they could trust her. So they took her into their confidence. Yes, they were the people the media spoke off. No, they were not violent and dangerous. They were a people carrying out a mandate their God had given them.

"What God? What mandate? You're not making any sense to me," interrupted Chante.

With the place now empty, she took the men downstairs and gave them fresh food. Taking up where they had left off formerly, the men continued as Chante listened intently.

They were passionate about what they believed in, and their lives sounded meaningful as they explained about their God, whose name was YHWH (Yahweh). They believed that He only was the One True God. They told her about Moses, of how great a prophet he had been, and about the laws he had received from YHWH – laws they were to follow and live by. But Moses had recently died, and their new leader, Daron, a fearless young man was determined to carry out the mandate YHWH had given to his predecessor.

Puzzled, Chante asked, "But what's that got to do with us here?"

With a serious look on their faces, the men replied, "Daron sent us to spy out your city."

"Why?" she asked in disbelief.

"Because your city belongs to us," continued the men with the same seriousness.

"Belongs to you? How? I have lived here all my life, just like my parents and all my ancestors. What do you mean?"

65

Dollys Y Crooks

"This city was promised to our forefathers. They failed to take it, and now it is left up to us to do it. Daron is determined that we will obey YHWH and take it. It is His will that we should live here."

The men spoke with such conviction that there was no doubt in Chante's mind they meant every word they said. Instinctively, she knew it was possible despite the media's flurry.

The sound of the whistling kettle broke into her thoughts. Chante rose from her chair, turned to the men, and said, "I know that you are going to take my city. Since I have saved your lives, will you also save mine?"

"Yes," they replied, "we will."

"What about the lives of my mother, my father, and my brothers and sisters?"

"Paint this place red," they told her. "Gather your family, and stay inside. When we come, we will spare it. Keep this a secret. If it becomes known, we will not be responsible for the outcome."

Conversation over, the men rose from the table and headed towards the door, while Chante made sure the way was clear. Quietly they slipped away into the night. Locking the door after them, Chante smiled to herself. "Don't tell anyone. It's a secret," the men had said. Those words were Chante's trademark. The strangers had nothing to worry about. Chante surely could keep secrets.

•

Preparing herself for bed, Chante pondered on the day's events. It had begun as another normal day in the House of Chante but ended as if she was watching a movie scene

Nightmares Tell a Story

with herself in the starring role. She ran her fingers through her hair – was it all a dream? Moving from the floor to the bathtub filled with her favourite scented bath oil, Chante continued to mull over the day's events.

Why did she ask the men to save her family, *especially* her mother and father, after all the pain they had caused her? Ever since she had opened the House of Chante, they had totally disowned her. She expected nothing less from them. Mother told her she had brought shame on the family's name and was a disgrace. But had her father not already done that? Which one of them had brought the greater disgrace?

Chante found it very difficult to understand her mother. Jaycinth had made her feel as though what had happened in her childhood was her fault – as if Daddy were the innocent party. How could she? Wasn't a mother expected to protect her children? Where was the "fight for your children" mentality a mother was supposed to have? Her father was the reason she had chosen this path in life; couldn't Jaycinth see that?

•

It was the strangers' words that caused a change in Chante's heart. In relating their history to her, they had told the story of a young boy named Joseph whose brothers were extremely cruel to him. One day they threw him in a pit and left him to die. Later, they changed their minds and sold him as a slave to foreigners heading to Egypt. Sometime later, the slave owner's wife accused him of attempting to sleep with her, resulting in Joseph being flung into prison.

Dollys Y Crooks

Chante had listened attentively and remembered thinking how cruelly life had turned out for such an innocent boy. The story continued that when Joseph was grown, he rose to prominence as Egypt's prime minister.

"Good for him," said Chante; "that will show those cruel brothers. What happened next?"

"There was a famine, and his brothers heard there was food in Egypt."

Spellbound, Chante had asked, "Are you serious? Did they meet him? Did they know it was him? Did he know it was them?"

"He knew it was them, but they didn't," replied the strangers.

"What did he do then?" Chante asked excitedly.

"He forgave them and was reunited with his father and the rest of his family once again."

•

Chante could not recall how the story of Joseph came into their conversation; she only knew that Joseph's choice to forgive his brothers for treating him so cruelly was now having a profound effect upon her. Did she have the '*faith*' to forgive the way Joseph did? Could she ever bring herself to truly forgive her parents?

As Chante lay back in the now-lukewarm water, the years of pain and shame flashed before her eyes. She saw herself, first as a shy young girl, then as a young adult and now as a full-grown adult and hated the person she had become. Bowing her head, Chante quietly prayed, "Strangers' God, please help me. I don't want to live like this anymore. Take away this pain, and help me do what the young Joseph

Nightmares Tell a Story

did in the story. Take this hatred for my parents away, and help me forgive them. Could You be my God as well as the strangers'?" Chante asked innocently.

Immediately, she felt as if a sharp dagger had sliced through her heart. Her heart, which had been closed and locked so long ago, was now being exposed. The concrete wall she had built up around it crumbled with each movement of the dagger. Instantly, her anger and hurt disappeared, and the spirits of lust, rebellion, and promiscuity that had controlled her life since childhood had no option but to instantly vanish.

Chante's heart was now clean, washed by the unseen Hands of the strangers' God. His love had banished her hatred and pain.

That night Chante tossed and turned, unable to sleep. This time, however, it was not due to nightmares. This time it was excitement. She could hardly wait for the sun to rise!

•

With renewed courage and a vision as clear as a bright sunny day with blue skies and no clouds in sight, Chante rang the doorbell to her parents' home.

Trembling, yet full of love and compassion, she waited for someone to answer. Jaycinth came and opened the door. In a voice barely above a whisper she said, "Come in."

Without another word spoken between them, Jaycinth left the door ajar and walked away. Chante entered her parents' home for the first time in a long while.

Errol was sitting reading the newspaper as usual, and as Chante entered, he looked up, put his head down again, and continued reading as though she were invisible. Choosing

Dollys Y Crooks

to ignore their cold reception, Chante sat down and excitedly relayed yesterday's events. Both parents sat still, neither wanting to make eye contact with their daughter. Undaunted, Chante continued.

After concluding her story, she knelt before her parents and said, "Dad, Mum, I forgive you of the past. I want you both to come with me. Please come with me."

Finally, laying his newspapers aside, Errol looked at his fourth child and wept, begging her to forgive him. Then, on his knees, he turned and asked his wife to forgive him too. Jaycinth reached over to Chante and for the first time since she had left home, Jaycinth placed her arms around her girl, her little girl and begged for her forgiveness.

Father, mother, and daughter cried in each other's arms as a new era began, banishing the nightmares of the past.

•

This story is found in Joshua, chapters 2 and 6.
The true characters are Rahab and the two spies.

•

Abuse comes in many different forms – mental, physical, emotional, and sexual. It leaves behind deep-rooted scars that mar our outlook on life and hinder our relationships.

Has someone abused you – someone you trusted? Forgiving the one who abused you is difficult, especially when the memories keep coming back time and time again and when physical scars are visible as proof. Yet forgiveness is the only way to be free from the pain and hurt caused by the abuse.

Nightmares Tell a Story

You see, by not forgiving but living in a place of hatred and bitterness (even though you are entitled to because of the wrong done), you are actually giving your abuser first place in your life. Are they really worth such a place of importance? You may say that I don't know the pain you feel. That may be true, but one thing I do know – God is the only person who should hold such a prominent place in your life.

Over 2000 years ago, Jesus hung on a cross with nails in His hands and feet for a crime He did not commit. Yet as He hung there, He prayed, "Father forgive them, for they know not what they do."

You see, forgiveness is not a feeling. It is a choice. It is not an emotion. It is a decision. Though some may have deliberately hurt you and intended to destroy you, if you will use the *law of faith* and trust God, He will turn it around for your good, just as He did for Joseph.

...whatever things are true, whatever things are noble, whatever things are just, whatever things are pure, whatever things are lovely, whatever things are of good report, if there is any virtue and if there is anything praiseworthy – meditate on these things.
(Philippians 4: 8)

Chapter 5

Tenacity under the Sentence of Death

Kezia was a Hebrew girl by lineage but was born and brought up in Goshen, Egypt, after her father Levi had migrated there with his ten brothers and their families. They had gone to join Uncle Joseph, who was the then prime minister of Egypt.

Daddy's family was quite a curious one for his dad had four wives and thirteen children between them. His mother, Carol, had the most – six boys and a girl. Daddy was the third eldest of all the children, and though his mother had given his father so many sons, it was no secret that she was not his favourite wife.

Grandma Carol had died long before Kezia was born, but she had heard many wonderful stories of how she cared for her children even though she was not favoured. It was this mental picture of her that Kezia grew up with. She often wondered what life would be like if Grandma Carol were alive today. Kezia vowed that when she grew up, she would

Tenacity under the Sentence of Death

be just like her, a woman of courage and strength who loved her children.

Daddy, together with Uncle Joseph and the rest of their generation, were all dead now, and Kezia was a grown woman, married, with two children of her own. Whenever she was unsure what to do, she asked herself, "Now, what would Grandma Carol do?"

•

From the time of Uncle Joseph's reign, life in Egypt had been good to them. Now, however, a new Pharaoh had taken control of Egypt. Disliking the Hebrews intensely, he brought fear to their hearts. They were too rich and too numerous, and should war break out, he was afraid they would side with Egypt's enemies.

Kezia and her people knew that their lives would change drastically, but they could not begin to imagine the magnitude of those changes. Swiftly, the new Pharaoh enacted laws that made it mandatory for all Hebrews to hand over their land and houses and displaced them to housing compounds. Losing everything overnight, they became slaves to the new king and to his regime. The Hebrew people were put to work on grand pyramid building projects and cities, supervised by cruel Egyptian taskmasters who made their lives bitter. Their children were barred from school and expected to work.

Then the king passed yet another law. This one sent more shock waves throughout the Hebrew community. It was aimed at Hebrew women, those about to give birth and those who had recently done so. Frightened and in great

Dollys Y Crooks

distress, the women could not believe that anyone could pass such a heartless law.

On every corner stood the edict, boldly embossed with Pharaoh's seal. They had never before experienced such fear.

EGYPTIANS!
You are commanded to kill ALL
boys born to Hebrew women.
Boys that have recently
been born are
to be thrown into the river.
The girls, you are to keep ALIVE.
By Order of Pharaoh

Now was definitely not the time for Kezia to be expecting her third child. The shock of the edict sent her into sudden labour. Silently, midwives made their way to the shabby quarters. Fear and confusion took hold of Kezia as she gave birth prematurely to a son. She turned her face to the wall and placed her hands over her mouth to stifle her screams, "No, no!"

In the darkness of night, the midwives crept stealthily away as Kezia decided this child they would not name. As the blood of young, innocent baby boys was being splattered

Tenacity under the Sentence of Death

all over the housing compounds of the Hebrew people, Kezia asked herself, *Where is this Jehovah that I have learnt about from childhood? Where is His strong arm, His love for His people? Why is He allowing this to happen to us?*

Though born in a foreign land, Kezia had been taught about Jehovah God and knew of His promise that a prophet would one day be born from among her people, one who would deliver them from oppression and set them free. Looking at her newborn son, she wondered aloud, "Could this child that is born in such a time of bloodshed be *that* deliverer?" Quickly she dismissed such an impossible thought from her mind. Then she recalled Grandma Carol and her tenacity to watch over her children, and she vowed that whatever it took to protect this child, even if it meant her own life, she would do it.

But what about the neighbours and the midwives? Would they bow under pressure and inform the authorities? What about friends who knew she'd been expecting a child? Would they turn her in?

Instantly, Kezia formulated a plan. She would dress him up as a girl! No one, apart from the midwives, must know that she had given birth to a son, at least until it was safe. *But will it ever be safe?* After discussing her plan with her husband, Abel, they called their two older children, Aaron and Mia, and sworn them to secrecy. Her household now settled, Kezia's thoughts turned to women she knew who were also expecting. What if they gave birth to boys? Had they too come up with a plan? Were they safe?

Sensing this child was indeed a special child, one with a destiny to fulfil, Kezia resolved to kneel daily and do the only thing she knew to do. She would call upon Jehovah,

Dollys Y Crooks

the God of her forefathers – Abraham, Isaac, and Jacob. She would ask Him for guidance and pour her heart and soul out unto Him.

•

Three months passed, and Kezia found it more and more difficult to keep up the pretence. Her baby boy was growing, and it was hard to keep him quiet. Then one day while on her knees before God, the thought of making a small basket using bulrushes came to Kezia. She would daub the basket with tar and pitch, and then place it into the river with the boy inside. But she would wait until the princess, Pharaoh's daughter, went down to the river to bathe, as was her custom; then she would float the basket in her direction.

It seemed a good idea at first, but Kezia began to have doubts. Why wait for the princess, the daughter of their enemy? The same king who'd passed the law to kill all the Hebrew boys. *If she finds out he is Hebrew, she will surely have him put to death.* Furthermore, this was the same river Pharaoh had commanded his people to throw the boys into.

"This doesn't make any sense," said a confused Kezia but then reasoned, "What have I got to lose? If I keep him here, he will die anyway."

•

Kezia found herself several days later doing exactly that: floating her youngest child, her second son, down the River Nile. Now, when she should be looking forward to seeing him turn his head and smile at the sound of her voice, to seeing his eyes watch her facial expressions, and to hearing

Tenacity under the Sentence of Death

him try to communicate, instead she was floating him down a river.

Powerful thoughts bombarded her mind. *Have I done the right thing? Did I really hear Jehovah God or was it my mind? Was it my heart and my emotions speaking to me? What will happen to him? Will he starve? Will he die?*

She walked away with tears in her eyes. Unable and unwilling to see the boy's fate, she told Mia, his older sister, to watch over him. Mia was a good girl. She would do a fine job.

As Kezia slowly made her way home, many memories came to her troubled mind, memories of Mia bathing, feeding, and hushing him to sleep under a blanket, when it looked like danger was near; the kisses and cuddles she gave him, and her laughter when he looked up at her face and smiled. Kezia even remembered the times she heard Mia pray to Jehovah, asking Him to protect her little brother and to save his life.

Whatever might happen, Kezia would content herself with these memories. She had prayed and asked God for guidance, and she chose to believe that He had shown her what to do. Pushing her doubts aside and wiping her tears away, Kezia repeated over and over to herself, "It was God who spoke to my heart. I know it was."

•

Finally, Kezia reached the front door of her home. She would pray again. While on her knees, she thanked Jehovah God for His answer, even though it didn't quite make sense to her. She thanked Him that her son was still alive, especially as many Hebrew women had given birth only to

Dollys Y Crooks

see their sons die by Egyptian hands. Kezia prayed that His peace would comfort them in these dark times.

Her attention turned again to her son, she thanked God that, although she had inherited the curse of great sorrow from Eve, she had found His new law – faith – and coupled it with the tenacity of her grandmother Carol. She was extremely grateful that not only could sorrow be greatly multiplied but so too could faith.

•

Kezia rose from prayer and busied herself with household chores in order to take her mind off the scene she had just left behind. As she was about to prepare lunch, there came a sharp continual knock on the front door. Her heart began to thump wildly. Had they found him? Had they brought him only to kill him in front of her? Slowly and cautiously, Kezia made her way to the front door where she could hear Mia shouting at the top of her voice, "Mummy! Mummy! Open the door!"

As she opened the door, Mia rushed in breathless. "Mummy, guess what?" Then her words became muddled and incoherent as she struggled to convey her story all in a rush.

Trying to calm her down, Kezia said, "Now, speak slowly so I can understand you. What happened to your brother? Why did you leave him?" Her voice rose to a pitch as she forgot the advice she had just given to Mia.

Excitedly, Mia replied, "Mummy, after you left, the princess saw the basket and told her servants to fetch it. When she opened the lid, he began to cry. I was so afraid and turned away. Then when I looked again, she was smiling and I heard her say, 'This is one of the Hebrew boys.' I ran

Tenacity under the Sentence of Death

to her quickly and asked if she wanted a nurse for him. She looked at me for a long time. Again, I was so scared."

Mia continued, "Then after what seemed like ages she just smiled again, this time at me. Mummy, it was as if she knew I was his sister. As I stood there trembling, she said very kindly, 'Yes, I would like a nurse for him. How quickly can you find one?' I gathered my robe and ran as fast as I could. Come on, Mummy, let's go!"

•

As Kezia followed Mia out the front door, forgetting to remove her apron, her heart was racing. Still, she battled with doubt and fear. Though she chose to believe that Jehovah God had answered her prayer, at the back of her mind came a torrent of questions once again.

Is the princess going to mock me? If she thinks Mia is his sister, she must surely know that I am his mother. Is she calling me to kill him before my eyes?

Again, as before, Kezia pushed away those awful thoughts whilst keeping up with Mia as they ran towards the River Nile. Seeking to allay her fears and to quiet her spirit, Kezia repeated time and time again, "He did hear me. I know He did. He inclined His ear towards me and heard me. Yes, He did. I know He did."

•

It was a nervous Kezia who reached the banks of the River Nile. Coming face to face with the daughter of her people's enemy, Kezia hesitantly returned the princess's knowing smile. With those two smiles exchanged between

Dollys Y Crooks

women both with maternal instincts, together, they entered a secret, unspoken covenant:

> Princess: *I know this child is yours, condemned to die under my father's law, but I will do my best to protect him and give him the life you are unable to.*

> Kezia: *This is my son, born under your father's death sentence for my people. Thank you for going against his command to save my son. May my God cause His face to always shine upon you.*

Asking Kezia to take care of the child until he was weaned, the princess went on to inform her that she would pay for his care. Had Kezia heard right? Did the princess actually say she would pay her for looking after her own son? In that instant, all Kezia's fears and doubts vanished. She knew everything was going to be okay. Jehovah had indeed heard her prayer. Not only had He heard her, but she now knew for sure that the idea to float him in a basket down the River Nile was His. She was so glad she had obeyed Him.

The princess's next words brought Kezia back to reality with a jolt. "Oh, by the way, I have named him Moses."

Cautiously, Kezia took the child and held him in her arms. Then she slowly walked away, not daring to take her eyes off him. The princess could name him any name she chose. He was *her* son, and he was alive! Moses would be safe from now on. No harm would come to him again, for God had arranged for him to be protected by a child of the very one who sought to destroy him. What a God!

Tenacity under the Sentence of Death

All day long, Kezia thanked Him that she had inherited her Grandma Carol's faith. She pledged to Him that as long as she lived, she would teach this child, this boy of destiny, the circumstances in which he was born –how he came into a world of bloodshed, mayhem, and destruction but was kept mightily by the awesome power of Jehovah God.

This story Kezia would rehearse in her son's ears time and time again.

•

This story is found in Exodus, chapters 1 and 2.
The true characters are Jochebed, her three children Aaron,
Miriam, and Moses, Pharaoh and his unnamed daughter.

•

Just two verses out of the entire Bible mention this woman's name, but what an impact she has had on the world through her youngest son, who was born under a sentence of death. The Ten Commandments God gave him are still being taught to and lived by people all over the world today, centuries upon centuries later. In fact, all of this woman's three children were firsts in their field. Her eldest boy became the first high priest of Israel and her daughter, its first prophetess.

What made her children great as she faded into the background? I believe it was her faith and tenacity. She obeyed and trusted God against all odds and against her own reasoning. She believed He would protect her son, and she placed that seed of faith into action by floating him down the River Nile.

God asks no less of us mothers today. When our children are in danger, when they have gone "off the track," so to

Dollys Y Crooks

speak, it is difficult and frightening for us. We clutch at many things in the hope that they will see sense and return, but God simply tells us to trust Him. He knows the very paths they take, and He is the only One able to bring them home when they go astray. He tells us He will watch over them, while we pray and constantly put Him in remembrance.

Regardless of the situation, regardless of where your children are now, He knows – and because He knows, He is able to do exceedingly far beyond what you ask of Him. God has great things in store for your children and mine, just as He had for Moses despite the circumstances of his birth. Yet it is only when we entrust our children into His care that He can work through them His divine purposes.

Jim Elliot, a martyred missionary to the Auca Indians, once wrote, "He is no fool who gives what he cannot keep to gain that which he cannot lose." Moses was born under a sentence of death. His mother let him go, and because of her awesome *faith*, Moses did indeed become the deliverer of his people, liberating them from Egyptian oppression. We can do the same for our children too.

Perhaps you don't have any of your own, but you can find someone else's child and help them fulfil their destiny.

Thus says the Lord:
"Refrain your voice from weeping,
And your eyes from tears;
For your work shall be rewarded, says the Lord,
And they shall come back from the land of the enemy.
There is hope in your future, says the Lord,
that your children shall come back to their own border.
(Jeremiah 31: 16–17)

Chapter 6

As Graceful as a Palm Tree

Skye was as beautiful as the meaning of her name, "Palm Tree." She was tall, resilient, strong in a gentle way, and graceful. Such was the beauty of this young woman, born to a king and a princess, that her only brother, Sonny, thought highly enough of her to give his only daughter her name.

•

It was easy to see how Jonathan fell in love with Skye. The only trouble was that he was her half-brother (the king's eldest son from his second wife). Her daddy, the king, had quite a few wives, Skye's mother being one of them.

Day by day, Jonathan looked at his younger sister and desired her sexually. The fact that she was a virgin appealed to him even more, for he would not only be the king's first son but her first as well. His desire grew until it was out of control. He ate and slept with the idea constantly, so that it began to possess him.

Dollys Y Crooks

Rather than consult an older, trusted counsellor for advice, he turned instead to his cousin Joshua. Unknown to Jonathan, Joshua was always looking for ways to bring shame upon the king's children. He envied all the privileges they had, because of who they were. As long as they lived, his father would always be known as the king's brother and Joshua, simply as one of the king's nephews. Now here was Joshua's ideal opportunity: Jonathan confessing his love, or more appropriately, his lust for his half sister.

Joshua smirked, while stroking his cheek. "Here's the plan," he announced to Jonathan. "Pretend to be sick. Then when your father visits you, ask him to send Skye to prepare you a meal. When she comes in, send the servants away and…."

As Joshua's perverted and evil plan unfolded before him, Jonathan squealed with delight, his eyes lighting up. "Awesome plan, Joshua!"

Their plan worked to perfection. Daddy came to visit him in his sickbed. Ignorant of the ordeal he was about to put his beautiful young daughter through, the king agreed to Jonathan's request for Skye to prepare a meal for him.

•

On her way to Jonathan's home, Skye's thoughts ran on the past few months. She had sensed something strange in the way he looked at her, and though she couldn't quite identify what it was, she knew he was behaving very strangely towards her. Whenever she was in his presence, she felt afraid, nervous, and uneasy. She purposed only to be near him when her real brother Sonny was around, but

As Graceful as a Palm Tree

today she had no choice. Daddy had told her to go, and she had to obey him.

As Skye knocked on the door of Jonathan's home, she shook the uneasy thoughts from her mind. Maybe she was imagining things. When she entered Jonathan's house, all her fear and trepidation vanished as she saw he was not alone. Visitors had come to see him on his "sickbed."

Surely, he won't dream of doing anything to me. There are far too many people here. Besides, he is the king's eldest son and has a reputation to maintain, Skye consoled herself and began the task she'd come to do. The quicker she achieved it, the sooner she would be able to leave.

Dutifully, she prepared his meal while he spoke with his guests. When it was time for him to eat, he said something about feeling really weak and politely asked his guests to leave. Skye struggled to hold on to the dish in her hands. Fear gripped her heart as the last of Jonathan's guests left, silently closing the door behind them.

"You may serve me now," Jonathan said. Slowly and cautiously, Skye drew near. Suddenly, he grabbed her, and the dish fell to the floor, spilling food everywhere. "Lie with me." he pleaded.

Skye struggled with every ounce of strength she could muster, her mind numb with fear. "No!" She screamed, "You are my brother!"

As Jonathan forced himself on her, even in her fear, Skye tried to control the situation, to somehow bring reason to her half-brother's madness. "This is not the way to go," she pleaded. "I am your sister, and you are my brother. If you do this, you will bring shame on the king and on every one

Dollys Y Crooks

of us." Clinging to a last hope, she tried desperately, "Why don't you ask Daddy to let you marry me?"

It was no use; Jonathan proceeded to rip her clothes apart.

Hoping against all hope and clutching at anything that came to mind, she pleaded with him to stop. But it was all in vain. Skye discovered through a very painful experience that when a man is consumed by lust, he cannot see, nor will he listen to the voice of reason. Jonathan, obsessed by her beauty, raped his young half-sister.

•

After it was all over, Jonathan came to his senses. He looked at Skye sobbing and bleeding, trying to cover herself with her torn garments. She looked a pathetic sight. He hated himself and hated what he had done to her; but it was too late. He should have been protecting her, not violating her womanhood.

His passion now turned to hatred. As Skye struggled to get up, wrapping her robe around her bruised body with tears running down her cheeks, Jonathan called for a servant and commanded him, "Throw her out and bolt the door!"

Again, Skye tried to reason with him. "Please, you can't throw me out after what you just did to me, please," she sobbed. "Please, Jonathan. Don't do this to me. Let me stay here with you."

True to her name, in the midst of the most terrible situation a woman could find herself in, Skye struggled to reason with her violator, trying to retain some kind of dignity. Was she not a king's daughter after all? Jonathan simply turned his back to her and looked out his window.

As Graceful as a Palm Tree

The servant was shocked at the princess's condition. Longing to help her and ease her pain, he could only bow his head as he approached her. Gently, he escorted the distraught princess, clothes tattered and torn, to the front door of her half-brother's home and did what his master had commanded him. As Skye fell to the ground like a heap of rubbish, waiting to be discarded, the servant simply bolted the door.

•

Losing her virginity this way was not how she had dreamt of as a young girl. She was Skye, one of the king's daughters, a princess who once had a promising future. She had looked forward to a great deal in life – entertaining suitors, attending court dances whilst wearing some of the most magnificent costumes … the list went on and on.

Now, despite the fact that she was still the king's daughter, she could no longer wear the garment of many colours that virgin princesses wore. Her life had drastically changed forever. No one would ever marry her now. She was soiled goods, tarnished and defiled, doomed to a life of shame and loneliness, through no fault of her own.

Discarded on her half-brother's doorstep, she arose and angrily tore what was left of her robe. Heavy laden with grief, Skye laid her hands on her head and slowly walked away. Where to? It didn't matter. Moments earlier, her future was bright as one of the king's daughters', now through the obsession of a lustful half-brother it lay shattered beyond repair. What else was there for her to do but die?

•

Dollys Y Crooks

Some time later Sonny found his sister wandering the streets in a daze, still with her hands on her head. A crowd was following her, whispering and pointing. Some laughed, barely recognizing the beautiful young princess, while others asked. "Is this not Skye, the king's daughter? What terrible thing could have happened to her?" Some even surmised, "I bet it has something to do with that half-brother of hers – that evil Jonathan! God help us if he ever becomes king!"

Oblivious to them all, Skye had continued to wander with her hands on her head. Sonny, rushing towards his sister, removed his cloak and covered her shame. Putting his arms around her, he tenderly asked, "Skye, what happened?"

Numb with pain, and in a world of her own choosing, Skye did not answer. In her faraway place, she thought she recognized the face but gave not the slightest clue that she knew who he was.

Sonny continued, trying his hardest to pull his sister back into his world. "Did Jonathan trouble you?" he asked. At the mention of his name, Skye's whole body shook violently, and tears streamed down her cheeks.

Gently, Sonny lifted her face to his and wiped his baby sister's tears away. Then he looked into her eyes, filled with pain, and declared, "Jonathan will pay for this, Skye. As surely as I live, he will pay!"

Unknown to Sonny, Skye did not hear any of her beloved brother's words, for she had returned to her newfound world. It was a world in which only one person existed: a young, happy, carefree, beautiful princess called Skye.

•

As Graceful as a Palm Tree

Sonny took his sister's hands in his and led her to his home. She would be safe now. He would take care of her. As they walked, he shielded her from the piercing stares of those who had gathered and followed her. He tried in vain to silence the guilt and anger that were erupting within him.

Sonny had seen the way Jonathan looked at his sister and told his father, the king, about it. His father merely replied that Sonny was envious of Jonathan, since he was the eldest and had privileges the others did not have. Seething with anger against his father for putting his sister in such a situation, Sonny longed to march into the king's presence and declare that Jonathan must hang for what he had done. But it was no use, he knew the king would not carry out judgement against his eldest son, especially as he was heir to the throne.

When the king discovered what had happened to Skye, his solution was to keep the two brothers apart. Sonny decided not to make a fuss. He would deal with his half-brother in his own way, in his own time.

Not a day went by when Sonny did not hate Jonathan for violating his sister. As she lived with him, her pain was a constant reminder. For his part, Jonathan kept far away from Sonny, fully aware of his rage. He knew what was in the heart of his brother. Had he not felt something in his heart too towards his sister, before he violated her? Whenever it was inevitable that the two met, though no words were exchanged between them, Sonny's eyes would always say, *Your day is coming!*

•

89

Dollys Y Crooks

Two years later, Jonathan's day did indeed come. It was the time of the year when the sheep were being shorn. Sonny invited his father and all his brothers to attend the sheep shearing festivities. The king, as Sonny knew he would, declined. So to put the second part of his plan into action, he asked if Jonathan could go. Suspiciously, the king eyed Sonny and asked why; Sonny replied that it was because the rest of his brothers would be attending. Still feeling uneasy, the king eventually relented in the face of Sonny's insistence.

Having secured Jonathan's attendance, Sonny commanded his servants to give him plenty to drink and then, when he was well drunk, to kill him in revenge for violating Skye. Chaos ensued as the servants carried out their master's commands. Sonny's other brothers escaped on their horses, and word was brought to the king that Jonathan was dead.

Sonny fled to his maternal grandfather's home. The king would not see his son for another three years. And Skye? She remained in her own little world until her death.

•

This story is in 2 Samuel, chapter 13.
The true characters are King David, his daughter Tamar,
and his sons Amnon and Absalom.

•

Have you, like the young girl in this story, been raped, molested, or abused? As her name meant "Palm Tree" – tall, resilient, and graceful in adversity, that's how the sovereign God of the universe sees you.

As Graceful as a Palm Tree

You may have asked this question many times: "If God is sovereign, all-seeing, and all-knowing, why did He allow this to happen to me? Why me?" There is an influence in the world we call sin, which works through and in each of our lives. Like Skye in the story, through no fault of our own, we can find ourselves in situations that cause us much pain, fear, and anxiety.

When we accept God into our hearts through *faith*, when we put our trust in Him, He gives us beauty for ashes. He turns our adversities into triumphs and causes all things to work out for our good.

God takes great delight and pleasure in showing the enemy of man's soul over and over again that what he left for dead, God, the Master Potter, picks up, cleanses, moulds, fashions, and then polishes and shows off as His jewels. Why don't you allow Him to show you off today as one of His *priceless jewels?*

> *"They shall be Mine," says the* Lord *of hosts,*
> *"On the day that I make them My jewels."*
> *(Malachi 3: 17)*

Chapter 7

Don't Mind What He Calls You!

All was calm in the Barton household. Ade, the couple's only child, was tucked up safely in bed fast asleep while Owen sat at the kitchen table waiting for his wife to bring his dinner. Suddenly, a roar could be heard shattering the stillness of the evening.

"How many times I have to tell you, woman. I don't like my food cooked this way!" growled Owen, throwing the plate at her. Barely missing her head, the plate broke into miniscule pieces as it hit the ground. "Pick it up!" he screamed.

As Desiree stooped to pick up the fragmented plate, she felt a violent blow to her right cheek. Reeling from the pain, she cried, trembling, "Owen, I'm sorry. I'm sorry. I'll try harder next time. I promise!"

"There ain't gonna be a next time!" he snapped.

Cowering in the corner of the kitchen floor and expecting another cruel blow, Desiree was surprised when it didn't come. Daring to raise her head, she looked around and saw that he had left the room. *Where did he go? Will he be back?*

Don't Mind What He Calls You!

As she swept up the fragments and tidied up the kitchen, Desiree reflected on her marriage. It was hard to remember a day when it wasn't like this. Seeing Owen sprawled out on the sofa, snoring away to his heart's content, Desiree relaxed a little, feeling the tension drain away. Fear, however, was never too far away.

Hopefully he won't be up until the morning, she consoled herself.

Tiptoeing past him, afraid of waking him up, she headed upstairs for the bathroom.

•

Lying in the bathtub, Desiree remembered her wedding day. If anyone had told her this was how her life would turn out, she would have scoffed at them. Yet this was the harsh reality of her life years later. After drying the tears from her cheeks as well as the water from her skin, Desiree slipped into her nightdress and headed for bed, pausing at Ade's bedroom door to make sure the child was still soundly asleep.

•

At the time of their marriage, Owen had a secure job and was making good money. Although not rich, they were quite well off, having no financial worries. Desiree remembered those days with fondness. She recalled when shopping (although she preferred to call it retail therapy) for the latest outfit was "mandatory" for some social event she was required to attend with Owen. She recalled how Owen used to wine and dine her. Once they had even

Dollys Y Crooks

entered a local contest and were voted "Couple Most Likely to Succeed." What happened? Where did it all go wrong?

During their courtship, she had noticed how Owen on a number of occasions became jealous when she spoke to other men; it didn't matter to him that some of them were her close cousins. Each time she brushed his actions aside, choosing instead to believe it was his way of showing how much he loved her.

Then two months into their marriage, Desiree just happened to say something Owen didn't like. *Whap!* She felt his hand forcibly across her face.

"Why did you do that?" she had asked him. Owen immediately apologized and promised never to do it again, but each time she said or did something he didn't like, that always seemed to be the outcome. Over the years, Desiree came to realize how empty his promises and apologies were. She came to view them as mere words with no truth in them.

•

Their two-year anniversary brought a beautiful baby girl into their lives. Owen named her Ade, which meant "royal," and for a while things were bearable. As Ade grew, she lived up to her name, for she was very graceful, and Owen absolutely adored her. She was "Daddy's girl," the apple of his eye. Slowly the slaps became fewer, and Desiree became more and more grateful for the child's birth.

Then tragedy struck. Owen lost his job, through downsizing. The company had made very little profit that year and sought to reduce the number of its employees. Owen was one of the first to be laid off. Fear, dread, and

Don't Mind What He Calls You!

hopelessness swept over Desiree – just when she thought things were improving.

•

Owen began to drink heavily and to gamble. Doing her best to support the family, Desiree found a part-time job as a receptionist in a local dental clinic. Many times she would put aside money for a certain bill, only to find that Owen had found it and gambled it all away.

The beatings started once again. This time it was not just the odd slap here and there. It was fist punches and lashing out with his feet. Owen took out all his frustrations with life on his wife. Not even his love for Ade could keep him sober and temperate. It was her fault he lost his job. Her fault he beat her up. She made him do it. After each beating, Owen would hug her and cry on her shoulder. He would tell her how much he loved her and beg her not to leave him. She and Ade were his world, and he would simply die if they were not a part of it. Many times Desiree asked herself, *Does he really know what love is?*

Daily, she struggled to keep up her "perfect family" image. She wore makeup to cover the scars and wigs to cover the clumps of hair Owen had pulled out with his bare hands. At work she smiled and gave others advice as they sought her help. But Desiree needed help too. She desperately needed someone to talk to. But she could trust no one. Everyone thought she had the perfect marriage, and over the years, she did nothing to dispel this view. No, she decided, no one should ever know the truth about her marriage. Whatever it took, she would continue to keep up the façade.

Dollys Y Crooks

•

One day as Desiree sat on the bed brushing the long, silky wig she had just removed from her head, she sighed heavily. "How long can I continue to live like this, I wonder?" Instinctively, she turned and looked at five-year-old Ade lying spread-eagled across her bed colouring in an activity book. Was it fair to bring her into the world like this? Shaking her head as if to free her mind from such thoughts, Desiree rose up to prepare not only supper but also her mind and body for whatever might follow supper.

As the years passed, the façade began to crumble. Physically, Desiree was exhausted. Mentally her brain had taken too many blows. She was finding it very difficult to function, first as a wife, then a housewife, but somehow never as a mother. As a wife she had tried everything, and nothing worked. Owen simply got worse. He had even started sleeping out.

•

One morning as Desiree dropped seven-year-old Ade off to school, she made the decision to leave the matrimonial home. "I can't live like this anymore. I don't care what happens. For Ade's sake, I must leave," she whispered as she bowed her head on the kitchen table and sobbed her heart out.

A week later, while Owen slept after a drunken night's binge, Desiree and Ade quietly left the home early in the morning, never to return. Where to? Desiree didn't care, just as long as it was far away from here, as long as it was a place where no one knew about her or her past. She left both her

Don't Mind What He Calls You!

employer and Ade's teacher wondering why they had not shown up for work and school the next day. She couldn't take the chance of telling them, in case Owen asked after their whereabouts.

There was not a cloud in sight as Desiree boarded a train, tightly clutching her daughter's hands in hers.

"Where are we going, Mummy? Why have you taken a suitcase?" Ade asked inquisitively. "This isn't the way to school. What about Daddy? Isn't he coming with us?"

Over and over Ade bombarded her mother with questions. To every question, Desiree replied gently, "It's okay, Ade. It's okay."

Finally, frustrated and exhausted, Ade fell asleep while the train roared on its way. Somehow, she sensed in her young mind that she would never again see her father.

Evening approached, and as the train crossed the border towards its final destination, Desiree found herself in the city of Tyre. Tonight, she would find a place with a bed that offered breakfast. Then after breakfast, she would look for an apartment to rent.

Next day, after a restful night's sleep and a hearty breakfast, Desiree set out with Ade. Finding several places she could afford, she chose a furnished home that was small but comfortable. Now settled into accommodations, Desiree's thoughts turned to seeking employment. She would rest for a few days with Ade while they got accustomed to their new surroundings.

A few days later, Desiree went from factory to factory seeking employment. She discovered that the city was famous for its purple-red dye. Tyrian purple, as it was known, was used to colour clothing worn by royalty and people of high

Dollys Y Crooks

ranking. It had brought the city much wealth, and because of this, factories were always in need of workers. Desire had no problem in finding employment during the hours Ade would be at school.

That night they retreated to their new home. Tomorrow, Desiree would look for a school for Ade.

The following day Desiree was able to register Ade in her new school, which was quite close to the factory where she would work. Desiree could not believe her luck. Things had worked out so well and she wondered, just wondered, whether Someone above was watching over them. Together they settled down in their new life, leaving the past far behind. Desiree had at last found peace of mind.

•

But something very strange was happening with Ade. Desiree noticed that she would sometimes sit and rock herself backwards and forwards for no reason at all. Foam would then emanate from her mouth and she would utter incoherent sounds. To cap it all, the voice with which she would utter those sounds was definitely not the voice of a seven-year-old girl. Most oddly, Ade did not seem to be affected by it in any way. In fact it seemed a very natural thing for her to do.

"How bizarre," murmured Desiree. "What is going on?" Feeling slightly afraid, she wondered what had happened to the peace of mind she had begun to experience. It seemed that every time things appeared to be going right, something always happened to shatter it. Wasn't it enough for her to have fled an abusive marriage and left her home behind?

Don't Mind What He Calls You!

What was wrong with Ade now? Why her? She was the one thing that brought her comfort and joy.

•

As Desiree retired to bed that night, memories of her life with Owen came flooding back. She had been so busy creating a new life for herself and Ade, she had hardly allowed herself to reflect on him. Was she subconsciously afraid to – afraid that he might be looking for them? Or worse, might find them?

She had tried hard to shield Ade from the cruel scenes back home, always putting her to bed before Owen came home. Painfully, she remembered the night he came home early in a drunken rage. As she rushed to put the child to bed, Owen stuck his foot out, tripped her over, then raped her in front of their daughter.

Desperately, she tried to shield the child. "Ade, go to bed!" she had shouted. "Go to bed! Mummy is coming soon to tuck you in, honey."

No sooner had she finished her sentence when, *whap!* – a blow to Desiree's head knocked her senseless. When she came to, Owen had fallen asleep on the floor, and Ade sat by her bedroom door crying.

Pushing thoughts of him out of her mind, Desiree focused on Ade. What should she do about her strange behaviour? Could the child having witnessed such scenes be the reason why it was occurring?

•

Dollys Y Crooks

Desiree spent the next month taking Ade from one specialist to the next after school. Each told her to try this or try that. Nothing worked, and the little money she had managed to save was gradually dwindling away. Sometimes, Desiree would go without food just to pay the bills. One day she read about a witch doctor who practiced under the guise of "alternative medicine." Many people with ailments and curses had tried it, and it appeared to have worked for them. Desiree thought she had nothing to lose by going there. She would take Ade tomorrow.

•

While Desiree was still deciding what to wear and Ade watched television, an announcement caught Desiree's attention.

"We interrupt this programme to bring you news of an extraordinary happening. The whole city is being turned upside down, and police have had to be brought in to keep crowd control. Apparently, a man called Jesus is healing the sick, opening blind eyes, and unblocking deaf ears. He is loosening the tongue of the dumb and casting out demons. It seems hundreds or perhaps thousands of people are bringing their loved ones to Him to be healed. Some are falling down frothing at the mouth, only to rise up in their right minds. Others are throwing their crutches aside while wheelchairs are being rolled away empty. Even more amazing, He is not charging for His services! What is going on?"

Two things attracted Desiree. He was casting out demons, and His services were free. She stood riveted to the television screen hungry for more information. Casting

Don't Mind What He Calls You!

out demons? Was that what was wrong with Ade? She did foam at the mouth.

"Maybe I should go there instead, especially if His services are free," Desiree said aloud. "Maybe He's the answer for Ade's strange behaviour. I know the place where He's meeting people."

Was there really anything free these days though? She wasn't sure, but she was determined that if it was, Ade would surely benefit from it!

Fully dressed now, Desiree turned to Ade and asked, "Ready?" The child turned and leapt on her suddenly with eyes blazing red and lips curled up at the corners. Using her fingers as claws, Ade lurched at her mother, scratching and clawing at her, all the while uttering unintelligible words. Swiftly, Ade had gained the strength of a full-grown man!

Desiree had to forget this was her daughter and fight with all her might. Memories of Owen pounding her body with blows flashed in her mind, and with strength as if from an unseen force, she defended herself against her seven-year-old daughter.

Then as abruptly as Ade had lurched at her mother, the child slumped to the floor, shrieking hysterically, "Mummy! Mummy!" Seeing her mother's scratched face, she asked sadly, "What happened to you, Mummy? Why do you have all those scratches on your face? Why are your clothes torn? Is Daddy here? Did he find us? Shall we run away again?"

Holding her gently, Desiree led her to her room. Wiping away the tears and listening to her daughter's fears as only a mother can, Desiree hushed her until, exhausted, Ade fell asleep in her arms.

Dollys Y Crooks

Things would be okay now. She would leave Ade alone for a few hours. If this man, this miracle worker, this Jesus was real, then this would be the last time Ade would ever behave like that. Quietly, Desiree slipped out the front door and locked it behind her.

•

The crowd appeared much larger than she had seen on television. Anything free would always draw crowds. Was that not partly her reason for being there too? As Desiree pushed past the crowds and caught sight of Him, something extraordinary happened. It was as if no one else were there, just the two of them. Then, somehow, she found herself motionless before Him. Weeping unashamedly, Desiree told Him all about Ade and pleaded with Him to help her.

"Please help me," she wept. "I know You can. I have seen the compassion You have for so many. Please help my daughter."

The Miracle Worker answered her not a word. In the silence that followed His silence, she became even more determined. Something about Him told her He was the One she needed and that He had all the answers. But though His services were free, what personal price was she willing to pay for them?

His security men seeing He did not acknowledge her, concluded He did not heal foreigners and promptly shoved her aside. "He has no time for you!" they shouted.

But Desiree knew they were wrong. She knew that though He spoke no words, His eyes told her: *Don't give up. Keep making a demand on Me.* She had come too far to care

Don't Mind What He Calls You!

about people and their prejudices. Her mission was greater than that. Her daughter's life depended on her.

Undaunted, she dusted herself off and tried again. This time, He uttered words that seemed only to reinforce the view of His security men.

"It is not right to take the children's food and give it to dogs."

The security men looked at her again, this time disdainfully, and told her in no uncertain terms, "Go away, and stop troubling Him!"

Desiree thought about the child she had left asleep at home, her only child, her joy and her comfort. She could not give up now. She was too close. She would use that same strength and tenacity she had found fighting off the demon in her daughter to fight *for* her now.

Instead of being offended at His reply, Desiree took a different stance. *Dog* was a name her husband had called her, amongst others, for so long that she reasoned to herself, "If this man can do what people say He can, then I can take Him calling me a dog and anything else He chooses to."

The crowd, silent at first, began to laugh and to mock. Finally, they chanted in unison, "He only heals His own, not dogs!"

Amidst the laughter and the jeers, Desiree calmly replied to His statement, "That's true, sir, but dogs eat the crumbs which fall from their masters' table."

Those close to Him, hearing her speak, grew silent. The rest of the crowd gradually hushed once more. What would happen now? His security men had never seen a woman like this before. None of their women would dare to be so

103

Dollys Y Crooks

bold. Then again, she wasn't one of their women. She was a foreigner.

Jesus, the Miracle Worker, looked at her and marvelled. In the midst of such a hostile crowd she had answered His statement with great conviction. A smile crossed His face as He spoke the words her ears had longed to hear from His lips the moment she had set eyes on Him – words of healing, comfort, and joy.

"Woman, great is your faith. That which you have asked of me is done. Your daughter is indeed well again."

Clinging to those wonderful words, Desiree held her head high and walked through the crowd as though they never existed. Foreigner or not, her mission was accomplished.

•

On arriving home, Desiree fumbled for the key to her front door. Eagerly placing it in the lock and forgetting to close the door behind her, Desiree ran breathlessly up the stairs to Ade's bedroom. Ade was still asleep and as she gazed upon her, her face radiated with joy and peace. It was again that of a seven-year-old child, soft and lovely. His words had indeed set her free. Desiree would never forget the Miracle Worker, for He had done so much for her and Ade. From now on, He would have a special place in her heart, and when memories of her past come flooding back, she would simply remind herself of this day.

•

Don't Mind What He Calls You!

That day, Jesus validated Desiree not only as a woman but also as a foreigner. He knew she had left an abusive marriage to begin life anew. He knew she had lost her self-esteem, her value, and her pride in being a woman. He knew there were days in her life when she had felt like a useless person, a worthless trash can.

By making reference to a *dog* publicly, He had triggered the memory of her husband's derogatory comments and brought her to a crossroads where she had a choice. Would Desiree continue to view herself the same way in this new life she was creating, or would she rise above it with a new mentality? The need for her daughter to be healed decided which road she would take.

By taking no offence to His words and answering Him as she did with such conviction, she proved that she no longer viewed herself the same way. Instead, her outlook was one of her eating, from His table, crumbs of grace, mercy, and love.

•

This story is found in Matthew 15: 21–28.
The true characters are Jesus, a
woman of Canaan, and her daughter.

•

Are you in the midst of a people who have placed limitations on your life because you are a woman or because you are of a certain colour or a certain race? Set yourself free! Jesus is Master of all. Though you may not be of the Jewish race and despite the prejudices, racism, and name-calling

Dollys Y Crooks

you have experienced, you can still place a demand on Him, on His time and His schedule, and know for sure that He will stop everything just for you.

You see, Jesus went to Tyre and Sidon *just* for her! After His encounter with her, He left the city and headed for the Sea of Galilee.

Just like her, Jesus knows your past. He knows you need to build your self esteem and self worth again. Though it seemed a strange way to do it, He wanted Desiree to realize that, regardless of her past, regardless of what blows life dealt her, regardless of how many limitations were placed on her, *through* Him, she could rise above them all.

He is waiting to do the same for you today. All you have to do is call upon Him.

Call upon Me in the day of trouble;
I will deliver you, and you shall glorify Me.
(Psalm 50: 15)

Chapter 8

All Cleaned Up!

nclean! Unclean! Joan had heard that word so many times before in reference to herself that she had even forgotten her real name. Each day she awoke with that word, and each night she went to sleep with it. Over the last twelve years, aside from her husband Winston, *unclean* had become her constant companion. Those twelve years seemed like a lifetime – a lifetime living under this curse; this hell on earth. To Joan that was what it felt like.

•

She had come from humble beginnings. Both her parents died when she was very young, and she grew up with her maternal grandparents. They looked after her with what little they possessed, and Joan had turned out to be a well-rounded young lady. She was not a stunning beauty but was gifted in many areas and had a wonderful personality. Many were drawn to her warmth and hospitality, for she had a lovely way of instantly putting people at ease.

Dollys Y Crooks

That's how Winston came under her spell. They had known each other since teenage years and were friends who shared many wonderful moments together.

•

Now they were married and had moved into their dream home, which they imagined would soon be filled with the laughter and cries of children.

However, one morning Joan woke up bleeding. She found this strange as she wasn't due to menstruate for another two weeks. She reasoned maybe it was the strain and excitement of moving into their dream home and buying new furniture and everything else that went with it.

Two weeks passed, and still Joan continued to bleed. A month passed with the same result. Her doctor could offer no reason why her flow of blood continued. She faithfully attended appointment after appointment, each time to be told no reason could be found. The couple searched themselves for reasons why. Was it something they had or had not done? Eventually, Winston took up residence in the spare room. For how long? Neither of them could say.

"Honey," Winston said to Joan one day, "we will go to the best specialists. If they are unable to help you, we'll go abroad. Whatever it costs, you'll be okay."

Winston smiled at his wife reassuringly, not daring to believe this illness that had come upon her so suddenly was incurable and that all the money in the world would not be able to cure her.

•

All Cleaned Up!

Years passed, and Joan's bleeding continued, with physicians unable to explain or improve her condition. She had tried many specialists, drunk every medicine, and swallowed every pill that was given to her, but still she continued to bleed. Depression set in as each visit, medicine, and tablet grew more expensive.

She often watched her husband; the pain on his face said it all. She was incurable. She would not be able to bear children for him. Little did she realize that his pain did not come from the fact she would never have his children; rather, it came from watching her waste away each day.

Some mornings she couldn't even raise herself out of bed. Gone was the cheerfulness in her voice and her loving ways. How Winston wished he could have his wife back again, even if just for a moment. For before him was a total stranger. She had lost so much weight that her face was sunken and her cheekbones protruded. There was nothing he could do to make her well again.

•

As Joan entered the twelfth year of her bleeding, the couple's entire savings were used up. All that remained was the dream house and the land on which it stood.

The truth came home to Winston with painful sharpness one day. Everything he had achieved in life meant nothing, for they were unable to heal the one he loved the most. Brave Winston. He had tried hard to be tough, to shoulder the entire burden of his wife's illness, never allowing her to see him cry or express grief. Each time she fell asleep, Winston would walk away hopeless and helpless, and when she was

Dollys Y Crooks

awake, he would keep the tears from flowing. Joan must never see him cry.

Life can be so cruel at times. It gives you riches; it clothes you in fine linen and feeds you sumptuously. Yet when certain sicknesses come knocking, life can find you no cure.

•

One morning Joan awoke to see that Winston was not by her bedside as usual. Each morning, the first thing she saw was his face. Where was he? Mustering up all her strength, Joan made her way to the spare room. Seeing Winston lying there with a peaceful smile on his face, her first thought was that he had overslept, but as she drew near and placed her palm on his cheek to stroke him, he felt awfully cold to her touch. Frantically she shook him and called his name, "Winston! Winston!" He made no move and no sound.

That was the morning Joan discovered that her husband – her friend, her comfort, her support – had died in his sleep. A broken heart and sheer exhaustion had taken him before his time. Joan sat and simply stared at her Winston, unaware of time passing.

How could life deal her another blow like this, in her condition? Was it not enough that she was bleeding with no cure in sight? Must Winston be taken away from her too? Could life really get any worse? The only conclusion Joan reached was that she must have done something really terrible for God to rain down His wrath on her like this.

Daily, Joan wished for death in order to join her husband. She missed him unceasingly. They had known

All Cleaned Up!

each other for so long that she wondered how she could live without him now. Joan wished that she had died and not Winston. Did he not stay and take good care of her? He could have divorced her and got on with his life. But not Winston. He had vowed that in sickness or in health, for better or for worse, for richer or for poorer, he would stick with her. He had shown to the very end that he took with utmost seriousness those vows he'd spoken so many years ago.

•

Alone and left without a husband or children, Joan thought of ways to kill herself. Then, as if sent by divine Providence, someone knocked on her door, interrupting her thoughts. Joan slowly turned her head and looked at the door.

Who can it possibly be? she asked herself. "Come in," she replied feebly.

In rushed her neighbour Andrea excitedly.

"Joan, there's a stranger just arrived in town. The whole town is buzzing with excitement over him. He's healing the sick, touching lepers, cleansing the unclean, casting out demons; some even claim He's the Messiah! I heard the dumb are speaking and the deaf are hearing. They say his name is Jesus."

As Joan listened intently to her neighbour's report, faith rose up in her heart, and a ray of hope seemed to light her from within. Forgetting all about wishing to die, Joan heard herself whisper, "Will you help me get dressed? Will you take me to where He is?"

Dollys Y Crooks

"I thought you would never ask," Andrea replied with a broad grin on her face.

Gently, but hurriedly, Andrea dressed Joan.

•

As they approached the place where Jesus was, they could not see Him, for hundreds of people were gathered around Him. Andrea held Joan's hands in her own and asked if she was okay. She feared that the multitudes of people, together with the heat of the sun, might cause her to lose her balance and faint.

In a voice so quiet, it was almost difficult to hear her in the crowd, Joan replied, "Yes, I am okay. Andrea, I must see Him today. I can't go another day like this."

She suddenly remembered her earlier thoughts of suicide. Too ashamed to share such thoughts with Andrea, she hastily brushed them away. Hands clasped together, both women continued to press their way through the crowd.

•

The crowd parted unexpectedly and fell into an eerie silence. From where they stood, Andrea could see James, one of the rulers of the synagogue. He had fallen prostrate at Jesus' feet. What could have possibly happened to cause such a proud man as James to humble himself like that in front of such a huge crowd? Word spread throughout that his only daughter was at death's door, and he had come to ask Jesus to heal her. Only trouble was, James lived in the direction opposite to where Jesus was heading. Would

All Cleaned Up!

Jesus change His mind? All eyes watched as Jesus changed direction and began to follow James.

As Andrea turned to discuss this sudden change of events, she discovered Joan had disappeared. Over and over again, she called her name, but to no avail. Where could she be? Had she fainted? Was she lost in the crowd? Had they trampled her? Andrea by this time was becoming frantic with worry when there was another unexpected surge in the crowd and a further eerie silence.

How peculiar that there should be so many people congregated in one place with such periods of unnatural silence. What had happened now? Did something happen to the One called Messiah, or had another prominent Jewish leader fallen at His feet?

Andrea, feverishly scanning the crowd for a glimpse of Joan, saw and heard the One they called Messiah turn and ask, "Who touched me?"

What an unusual question to ask with so many people pressing around Him. A few seconds later the crowd erupted into laughter. They too thought it was a strange and humorous question to ask.

One of Jesus' disciples, a rough-looking bearded man said, "Master, how can you ask such a question when there are so many people here? Surely hundreds have touched you since we began our journey."

Messiah turned to face him. In a stern yet un-condemning way almost as though wanting to recognize and commend the one who touched Him by faith, He replied, "Somebody made a demand on my power."

Remembering Joan, Andrea fervently resumed her search. Where was she? Andrea could not believe her eyes.

113

Dollys Y Crooks

Joan was stooping at His feet! However had she got there, and what was she doing in such a position? Andrea could only look on in awe with everyone else. Did His question have anything to do with her neighbour kneeling at His feet? Sensing her fear and knowing her feeble condition, Andrea moved closer to Joan in spite of her own fear. Joan needed to know someone was on her side.

With hands trembling, head bowed and a voice barely above a whisper, Joan confessed to touching Him.

"I was the one who touched You. I have had this sickness for twelve years now, and no one could help me. I have tried everything. Then my neighbour told me about You. She told me that You heal the sick and cleanse the unclean. I did not want to trouble You. I thought if I could only get close to You, if I could only touch You, perhaps I too could be cleansed by Your power. Then as You changed direction and began to follow James, I *had* to reach for Your cloak and touch it. And as I did so, I felt something leave my body, a calm came over me, and I knew I had been healed and cleansed. Please forgive me for touching Your cloak."

Joan, Andrea, and the crowd waited with bated breath to see what would happen next. The man they called Messiah bent down, took both her hands in His, and pulled her up to face Him. Joan immediately shied away from His touch. Covering her face with her shawl, she shook her head vigorously, beckoning Him to leave her alone.

Jesus instead drew her gently towards Him. Removing the shawl from her face, He said in the presence of all, love and compassion filling His voice, "Daughter, be happy. Your faith has healed you. Go home in peace."

All Cleaned Up!

A wonderful glow crossed Joan's face as she experienced for herself Jesus' loving touch. Andrea could only marvel at the remarkable change in her neighbour's countenance and stature. Gone was Joan's stoop; now she stood upright. With tears in her eyes, Andrea hugged her and, with a smile as wide as a crescent moon, declared, "All that we have heard of this man is true. He must be the Messiah!"

Both women walked away that day with tears streaming down their faces. Joan was elated. After all these years, she was finally healed. She could resume her life again. She was no longer "unclean." Now, she was clean.

A shadow crossed her face as she thought about Winston. She missed him so much. He had taken such good care of her over those terrible and trying times. How poignant that he had not lived to witness this miracle that happened to her today.

•

Where others had failed, the One they called Messiah succeeded. Joan wondered whether He had known of the turmoil she had faced that very day and her thoughts of taking her own life only moments before meeting Him. Did He know she needed desperately to regain her confidence and self-esteem? She felt He did. Had He not used the intimate term and called her *daughter* as a father would his child? He'd reminded her that even though she had been unclean for twelve years, she was still a daughter of God. She was God's child; a daughter of the Covenant He had made with Abraham, her father of faith centuries earlier.

Joan came to realize that God was not raining down His wrath on her and that by drawing her actions to the attention

Dollys Y Crooks

of the crowd and then commending her for her faith, Jesus truly showed an amazing act of love and compassion.

Was He or was He not the Messiah? Joan only knew that He had set her free from twelve years of sheer hell. Now she had every reason to live and not die. She had every reason to rebuild her life, to laugh, and to fall in love with the world all over again.

•

This story is found in Luke 8: 41–48.
The true characters are Jesus, the woman with
an issue of blood, and Jairus.

•

Are you in need of healing for your body, mind, or emotions? Do thoughts of suicide or self-mutilation plague you? Are you always depressed and unable to see the way out? Many times life deals us cruel blows, but there is a God who comforts and guides us through those blows. He has said that if you will come to Him and believe His word, He will never leave you nor abandon you.

He is known as the Divine Healer, the Greatest Physician, and the Awesome God. It makes no difference what category your sickness falls into – physical, mental, or emotional. He heals them all.

What do *you* have to do? Just like the woman in this story, believe that there is none who loves you enough to heal you completely and give you a fresh start in life – none, that is, but Jesus. It is so simple, yet sometimes we make it so very difficult.

All Cleaned Up!

We spend all that we have going from one specialist to another, and although people have accumulated the knowledge to cure many kinds of diseases, sometimes it takes more than knowledge. It takes *faith!* When life doesn't seem fair, keep going. Don't give up; your circumstances can't last. Do as Joan did – touch the Master!

And Jesus went about all Galilee, teaching in their
synagogues, preaching the gospel of the kingdom,
and healing all kinds of sickness and all
kinds of disease among the people.
(Matthew 4: 23)

Chapter 9

First, but Still Not Loved

Rakaya lived at home with Mummy, Daddy and younger sister, Iyana. Being the firstborn, she was the centre of attention to not only her parents, but her extended family also. However, three years later Iyana was born, and Rakaya paled in her shadow. This is Rakaya's story.

•

Rakaya had no beauty to speak of, while Iyana was very beautiful. As a child Rakaya often wondered why the difference for they both came from the same mother and father. *Iyana, Iyana, Iyana*, that was all she ever heard.

"Rakaya, how come you look like this and Iyana like that? Are you really both sisters, or were *you* adopted?" It was no use answering the taunts.

Rakaya decided nothing was ever going to change and that God was a very unjust God. He could have at least shared beauty out evenly or given her just a little bit. To add

First, but Still Not Loved

insult to injury, did He have to give her crossed eyes too? God was truly unfair, Rakaya mused.

Now that they were both grown, marriage was a big issue. Girls her age were either married or engaged. Rakaya always found herself in the role of bridesmaid but never the bride. Not only did she have to struggle with her looks, now no one wanted to marry her. What was to become of her? There were times she wished she hadn't been born. Rejection was second nature to her. The only person she could truly count on was Daddy. She was his girl. Sometimes she wondered though whether he really did love her, or whether it was pity he felt. Never mind, someone at least cared about her.

•

One day, a young male cousin from far away came to stay with them for a while. As expected, he fell in love with Iyana. Cousin Ricky decided to stay and work with their father.

"How much would you like me to pay you?" Daddy asked slapping cousin Ricky's shoulders in jest.

Shyly and with his head bowed to the ground, cousin Ricky replied, "I will serve you seven years for Iyana."

Daddy thought about his request for a while, then rubbed his hands against his beard and replied, "I suppose it is better to give her to you than to another. Okay, agreed."

The men shook hands and went their separate ways.

Iyana came rushing to Rakaya excitedly with news of Ricky's request and Daddy's approval. On and on she went about what Ricky said or didn't say, what Daddy did or didn't do.

Dollys Y Crooks

"What's new?" Rakaya said with a shrug, trying hard not to allow feelings of rejection to envelop her once again.

●

Rakaya had reached the age of marriage, and her father had not yet found a suitor. The fact that someone was prepared to work seven years of his life to marry her younger sister was very painful. As Iyana continued her story, insensitive to her older sister's feelings, Rakaya suddenly remembered that in their culture, the younger daughter never marries before the elder. A warm feeling rose up within Rakaya, and she entered into a world of her own, oblivious to Iyana's words. She clung to a glorious thought: *Iyana will have to wait on me to get married first, no matter how long it takes. Daddy will never put me to shame by allowing her to marry first, never!*

Iyana could continue her story all night, but Rakaya knew better.

As Rakaya watched Ricky go about his daily duties, she would often say, "He is so handsome. If only he loved me instead of Iyana. If only it was my hand in marriage he asked for and not hers. If only … if only …."

Then entering the real world again, she would sharply remind herself that it *was* Iyana's hand in marriage Ricky was working for, not hers. Bitter tears then flowed unceasingly down her cheeks. No one loved her. No one wanted her. *Surely, God, you can't be that unreasonable?*

●

The years passed, and preparations for Iyana's wedding came all too quickly. Mum, Dad, the servants, and Iyana

First, but Still Not Loved

were all very busy. "I might as well look busy," Rakaya sighed, secretly hoping her father had a plan for his eldest daughter. The shame this wedding would bring on the family if Iyana got married first was too much for her to contemplate. Had Daddy forgotten the cultural aspect of this wedding thing? Or was he so engrossed in the festivities? *Daddy, come on, where's the plan?*

Iyana's wedding preparations continued to proceed smoothly with still no word from Daddy.

•

Finally, Iyana's wedding day came. Celebrations were in full swing, and everyone was having a great time. Music was playing, and the guests were dancing and singing. There was plenty of laughter, eating, and drinking.

Rakaya was trying her hardest to be pleasant on the best day of her younger sister's life, despite the unkind comments that came her way. She was a picture of composure on the outside while internally screaming, *Daddy, come on! There's still time before they consummate the marriage!* She was desperate.

Then just as Iyana prepared to enter the bridal room where the marriage was to be consummated, Daddy beckoned Rakaya to come forward. As she knelt before him, he whispered in her ear, "Put on your veil and enter the bridal room."

"Daddy!" she protested, though not too convincingly. "This is Iyana's wedding day, not mine. Have you had too much to drink?"

She had almost given up on her daddy coming up with a plan, but this was suicide.

Dollys Y Crooks

"Where is Iyana?" She was sure she had seen her heading for the bridal room.

"I know what I'm doing – trust me. Now go in!"

Rakaya rose and nervously entered the bridal room, her mind in turmoil. *What if Ricky finds out that I am not Iyana and refuses to consummate the marriage?* The shame would be worse than not being married at all. What plan was this that her father had come up with?

A sudden thought turned Rakaya's fear to excitement. For the first time since Iyana was born, Rakaya would be first again. She would receive something before Iyana, even if it was obtained deceitfully. Rakaya knew her daddy wouldn't have let her down. He was always on her side, always looked out for her when others didn't. She knew she could depend on him every time there was a need.

With renewed courage, Rakaya entered into the bridal room as seductively as she knew how and climbed into the bed of consummation. Tonight was her night. This was what she had dreamt of as a young girl. Whatever might happen in the morning, tomorrow, next week, she didn't care, tonight was all that mattered. Once this marriage was consummated, Ricky would be her husband, and she would be his wife. His first wife! Nothing but death would change that.

•

The morning came too soon for Rakaya. All night she had not spoken a word to Ricky and tried to sleep with her face away from him. Now she awoke to find herself facing him. Too late! Ricky realized the woman in his bed was not the one he had worked seven years of his life for. He had

First, but Still Not Loved

been tricked. Uttering not a word to her, he got dressed and stormed out of the bridal room in anger. Rakaya lay on the bed, as still as a corpse, not daring to move.

What will happen now? she asked herself.

"Leave it to Daddy," a soft, gentle voice whispered. "Leave it to Daddy."

For Rakaya, that seemed to be the best answer in such circumstances. At that precise moment, Iyana crossed her mind. *I wonder what she's doing now.*

After what seemed like a lifetime, Rakaya's father and her husband entered the bridal room. Ignoring her presence, Daddy informed Ricky: "We have a custom here in our country. The younger never marries before the firstborn."

"Why didn't you tell me that *before?*" Ricky demanded.

"Stay with her for a week as her husband," pleaded Rakaya's dad. "Work with me for another seven years and I promise I will give you Iyana. My promise will only be conditional upon you fulfilling Rakaya's week."

"How do I know you will keep your word?" Ricky asked.

"If you want Iyana, you will have to trust me."

Imagine your father bribing a man to stay with you and as a reward he could have your younger sister. The rejection Rakaya felt was hard to bear.

"I guess that's the price you pay for deception," said Rakaya, comforting herself. Sadly, she turned her head so her tears would fall on the pillow and not on her cheeks. Who was she fooling? He had spent seven years working for her younger sister, not her, and to prove how much he really loved her, he was willing to work for another seven years.

Rakaya concluded this was worse than being unmarried. The hurt was greater than any she had ever known before.

Dollys Y Crooks

She might be Ricky's first wife, but she was still unloved and unwanted, still doomed to walk in Iyana's shadow. She was the first to be born and first to be married but still hurt, lonely, and unhappy.

•

If there was a God, as she had been taught, then He must truly be a one-sided God! What had she ever done to Him? How could He allow her to suffer like this? – to feel so much hurt and pain when her sister seemed to have everything she desired. Where was this God? If she could find Him, she would let Him have a piece of her mind. She would tell Him that He surely needed to make some changes to her life.

As if this unseen God had heard her cry, Rakaya gave birth to a son nine months later. Her husband now had an heir. Again she was first, for her sister Iyana had so far been unable to conceive. Was this God showing her that He cared about her too, even though it seemed to her that He had forgotten her? Was He telling her that it was her turn now, her time, her season?

Rakaya smiled as she held her newborn son in her hands. "God has heard me," she said. "Surely, my husband will love me now, for I have given him a son to continue his lineage into the next generation."

Each time Rakaya produced a son, she hoped the child's birth would bring Ricky closer to her. By the time she had borne child number four, whom she named "Praise," she realized that a child does not cause a man to love you, if he did not love you in the first place. Sadly, she came to understand that, though Ricky might care for and even have

First, but Still Not Loved

a fondness for her, his heart was always and forever would be sold out to Iyana.

God had given her so much joy and laughter through these her four sons. She would always praise and thank Him for that. For now, she would content herself and stop trying to compete with Iyana.

A few more years passed, and Rakaya went on to bear Ricky two more sons and one daughter.

•

As Rakaya reflected on her life, she saw that she had much to thank this "one-sided" God for. She never thought she would be married, let alone bear seven children. From now on, she would try her hardest to forget her childhood memories of rejection. Instead, she would live for the present, through and for these children He had given her.

Iyana died giving birth to her second child on the return to Ricky's hometown, and Rakaya went on to score another first, for when she died she was buried with Ricky in the family tomb. Her legacy lived on through her six sons, for they were the major part of the twelve tribes we know today as the nation of Israel.

•

This story is found in Genesis, chapters 29 and 30.
The true characters are Leah, Rachel, Jacob, and Laban.

•

Can you identify with this story? Many women have children hoping that a man will stay with them. Some have

Dollys Y Crooks

children for many men, thinking, "This one will love me," whilst some believe that children will build their self-esteem and confidence.

Time and time again, we see the hurt this mentality produces. Many times the woman is left alone with hungry mouths to feed and no means of support.

Through my own experience, I have discovered that when you love and place value on yourself, you will see things differently and not accept just anyone or anything. You will look for a man who is selfless in his love, and you will be able to embrace and return such a love. Though it may take some time, trust God and wait on Him. You may think it's too late for you, but it's never too late with God.

Meanwhile, as you are waiting, the Bible tells us that God loves you so much that He sent His only Son to die on the cross (John 3: 16). Now that's love! If you have not experienced this love, why don't you make that step?

How precious also are Your thoughts to me, O God!
How great is the sum of them!
If I should count them, they would be
more in number than the sand;
When I awake, I am still with You.
(Psalm 139: 17–18)

Chapter 10

Watch Your Mouth!

Abbie rushed out to the courtyard, "Daddy! Daddy! You are home. Thank God you are back safely."

Seeing his only child, and hearing her voice so full of joy and laughter, Baldwin stood paralysed. Then in one swift movement, he tore his cloak.

In their culture, the tearing of clothes was a sign of grief, sadness, and mourning. The look of horror on her father's face, coupled with his actions, told Abbie something was drastically wrong. But what could be wrong? He had just returned from the greatest victory of his life.

"What's wrong, Daddy?" She cried. "Are you wounded? Are you hurt? Why are you so sad on such a great day of victory?"

It seemed to her as though someone had pressed a pause button. After what seemed like ages, Baldwin eventually turned to his only child and said with tears in his eyes, "My daughter, you have brought me much pain this day."

Baldwin slowly walked past her as if in a dream. It was then that Abbie ran to her "sad" room. As an only child she

Dollys Y Crooks

was often left to amuse herself, and whenever she felt sad or something was troubling her, she would always retreat there.

•

Abbie had developed this habit when they lived in Tob on a farm. Her place of retreat was a special corner in the barn. Daddy called it "Abbie's Corner" and could always find her there when she could not be found anywhere else. When they had moved to Mizpah in Gilead, there was no barn, so Abbie's special place was a "sad" room.

Here Abbie sat lost in her thoughts. Why had her father spoken such harsh words to her? What did she do? She hadn't seen him for quite some time and was happy to see him safe and not injured in any way. Why was he behaving so strangely?

•

From the time Abbie was able to understand, Baldwin had openly shared his life with her, especially his younger days. He hid nothing from her. Her paternal grandfather was a married man, and her father was born out of an adulterous relationship. His mother had handed him over or more accurately, dumped him on the porch of his father's home. It wasn't his fault he was born under those circumstances and after all, it did take the two of them to make him.

Daddy's life with his father's wife and her sons was sheer hell. He'd looked forward to the day when he would grow up and become a man. He would leave, live his own life, and never look back. He couldn't say his father had done him any wrong. He had tried his best in a bad situation,

Watch Your Mouth!

but he looked much like his mother, and this often brought conflict in the home, serving as a reminder of his father's philandering ways.

As for his mother, he had never seen her. She never once visited him, and his father never took him to see her. The feeling was mutual: he had no wish to see her either. That was the past, he had told Abbie. His mother made the decision to give him up and never to look back, so why should he go looking for someone who had no wish to be found? Though he had said those words so sternly, Abbie could hear the sadness in his voice and see it in his eyes. She felt sorry for him, but what could she do? Cuddling up in his arms, she had vowed to love her daddy, even if no one else did.

•

As a child, her father had listened as his dad told the boys numerous stories of Israel's heroes and their exploits. Baldwin particularly liked the stories of Daniel in the lions' den and the three Hebrew boys who were thrown into the fire by wicked king Nebuchadnezzar. Now, as a grown man, he often repeated them to her. It made no difference to him that Abbie was a girl and might have preferred more romantic stories. Abbie smiled.

He had shared with her how, as a young boy listening to those stories, he would often dream of becoming a hero too. Then people would have to look up to him. No longer would they see him as the boy born out of an adulterous relationship or call him names like "that half-child of Simon's." No, they would have to show him respect and honour.

Dollys Y Crooks

Baldwin had told her how his life was made a little easier through those daydreams because when things got really tough, he would retreat into them. *That's why I have a special place that I retreat to*, Abbie said to herself. *I am just like my daddy.*

•

As the years rolled by and Baldwin's father grew older, his stepbrothers threw him out of the house; their father being too frail to intervene. They were afraid that their father would give him part of their inheritance – or worse, all of it.

Baldwin found himself in a town call Tob and made himself quite a name. Everyone knew him. From a child he had always had a wonderful personality, despite the circumstances he grew up in. When he became a man, nothing changed: he drew people to himself like a magnet. He even had a reputation as a tough guy. Men followed him and looked to him as their leader. Only trouble was that they were all disgruntled and "angry with the world." Baldwin had arrived; his boyhood dreams had finally materialized, and he was a hero. For that he gave his stepbrothers thanks.

To Abbie, her daddy was simply the best. She didn't care what anyone said about him. She loved him, and in her eyes, there was no one like him anywhere in the world. He was and always would be her hero.

•

Lost in her thoughts and unaware of time passing, Abbie let her mind wander further still. She remembered the day

Watch Your Mouth!

some strangers visited their home in Tob. Her father said they were his brothers and introduced her to them. She had never seen any of her father's family prior to this day. What could they possibly want after all these years?

After being introduced, Abbie quietly left the room but kept the door ajar, eager to eavesdrop on their conversation. They told her father that they had heard what a brave and mighty man he had turned out to be. Did he know, was he aware, that the country would soon go into battle with their age-old enemies?

From where she was hiding, Abbie could see her dad nodding. She also saw the smirk that crossed his face as his brothers continued: "Would you lead us in battle against them?"

She clapped her hand over her mouth to stifle a gasp which would have told everyone she was nearby listening to their every word.

Baldwin laughed aloud in their faces and retorted, "Weren't you the ones who made my life hell? Didn't you hate me growing up amongst you? What was it you said? Ah, yes, I remember, 'Daddy should have disowned you for the shame you brought on the family name' – as though any of it was my fault. Then eventually you threw me out. Why am I suddenly needed after all these years?"

The brothers hung their heads in silence, unable to justify their past actions.

Baldwin continued, "If I return with you and the Lord delivers our enemies into my hands, can I be your head?"

"The Lord is a witness between us and you if we do not do as you say," they replied.

Dollys Y Crooks

A satisfied look crossed Baldwin's face; he had them right where he wanted. After all the years of torture and pain, the tables had finally turned. Who was bowing down to whom now? Who needed whom now? Agreeing to lead them into battle against their mutual enemy, he sat down with the men to formulate their strategy. Eventually they rose up to leave.

Before they could reach the door, Abbie hurriedly tiptoed away.

•

Baldwin called Abbie and excitedly relayed the conversation he had had with his brothers. Abbie, of course, pretending all of it was new to her, asked, "Daddy, will we have to leave Tob?"

"Yes, very soon," came the reply.

It was with mixed feelings that Abbie prepared for the journey to Gilead, her father's place of birth. She loved the farm, the animals, and the way of life Tob had afforded her. She would truly miss "Abbie's Corner" in the barn. But if Daddy had to move to fulfil his life's ambition, she would move too. She was forgetting, of course, that as a young teenager, she had absolutely no say in the matter.

•

As they approached Gilead, Abbie's mixed feelings merged into excitement and fear – excitement at the thought of starting a new life, and fear about how her father's family would treat her. After all, the circumstances of his birth hadn't changed despite the fact that he was here to lead them

Watch Your Mouth!

into battle. Abbie abated her fears by consoling herself that things should be a lot better now, since they needed him so desperately.

Finally arriving at their new home in the town of Mizpah, Abbie couldn't believe her eyes. Standing before her was the biggest house she had ever seen. Turning to Baldwin and suddenly regaining a voice that had been lost since childhood, she squeaked, "Daddy, this is *our* house?"

Baldwin nodded, laughed, and then hugged her. "Yes, we will be happy here," he said, ruffling her hair.

Abbie spent the next few days giving each room a name. "This is such fun," she laughed as she whisked in and out of every room. There was the sleeping room, the eating room, the sewing room, and – oh yes, mustn't forget the "sad" room.

•

The day soon drew near for her daddy to lead the country's army into battle. Abbie had been especially careful to obey all of her father's requests. She did not want him to have to worry about her as well as winning a war.

As Baldwin headed towards the front door, Abbie hugged him and told him he was the best daddy in the whole wide world and that she would pray for God to bring him back to her with no injuries. Baldwin smiled, returned the hug, and said, "You are the best daughter any father could ask for."

Abbie watched Baldwin leave for battle that day. Then, as the car whisked him out of her sight, she ran to her "sad" room. There she prayed and asked God to bring her daddy back to her. She reminded Him that he was the only one

Dollys Y Crooks

she had and that furthermore, she was the only one on earth who loved him so very much.

Abbie arose from her knees and began tidying up. God had heard her prayer; she was sure of that. Making up her bed, she mused on how she and her father both had this "mother" thing in common. Her mother had died in childbirth, leaving her father to take care of her. But then Abbie reminded herself, Daddy's mother was alive – somewhere.

•

Weeks later, news reached Abbie that the troops had won the war. Daddy was on his way home! She hurried to prepare his favourite meal and to make sure the water was hot for him to bathe. Outside, she could hear the dogs barking. She must remember to chain them up so that when Daddy came through the gate, instead of the dogs greeting him, her face would be the first he would see.

Hearing the sound of a car pulling up towards their home, Abbie rushed out to the gate screaming excitedly, "Daddy! Daddy!"

It was then that he acted so strangely. She had prayed and asked God to bring her daddy home safely and He did. She could see he wasn't hurt or injured. Then why was he so sad, and what did he mean by saying that she had brought him much pain?

•

As Abbie continued to ponder these questions, the door to her "sad" room gradually opened, and Daddy entered.

Watch Your Mouth!

He knew exactly where to find her. With tears and sadness in his eyes, Baldwin sat down, placed his strong, safe arms around his only child and explained the reason for his great sadness, as he gently stroked her hair.

•

After his brothers had left that day in Tob, he made a vow to God. He told Him that if He would let him to win the battle, if He would vindicate him in the eyes of his brothers and those who'd told him he would amount to nothing and would become just like his mother, then he would give to God the first thing that came out of his house to greet him when he returned.

"My daughter, you were far from my mind when I made that vow. Not you, the apple of my eye, the one who brings me so much joy. As I watched my brothers bow down to me, I wanted revenge for the pain of my childhood. It felt so sweet to have them beg me. This 'brother' who they had hated so much would now become their leader."

As Baldwin finished his explanation, he separated himself from Abbie's embrace and wept, asking her to forgive him. Then slowly he made his way to the huge window of her "sad" room and looked out as though nothing in the world mattered anymore.

Abbie had never seen her father in such a state of grief, even when he spoke of his mistreatment by his father's family. Trying desperately to ease his pain and guilt, she said, "Daddy, it's not your fault. I chained the dogs up. You always tell me to let them roam free, but I didn't want them to be the first to greet you. I wanted to be the first. I wanted

Dollys Y Crooks

my face to be the first face that you saw. If I hadn't disobeyed you, they would have been the first to meet you."

Baldwin sadly made his way back to his daughter's side. "No, my daughter, it has nothing to do with you. It's not your fault. I got caught up in the heat of the moment and made a rash vow – a vow that stemmed from the rejection I experienced in my childhood. I have always wanted revenge over my father's sons, and blindly I made the vow without thinking of the possibilities. You were never a part of the vow I made."

•

He had brought her up to honour vows and to keep her word, even when it hurt. Though she had not made this vow, it involved her. The bond between them was too strong for Abbie to disobey her father and for Baldwin not to keep his vow.

Sitting in her "sad" room, with her father's arms around her once again, Abbie quietly said, "Daddy, if you have made a vow to God, then you must keep it. He kept his part. He gave you what you asked for and He gave me what I asked for."

•

Father and daughter sat together in the "sad" room: a daughter in the loving arms of a father she knew to be the best in the world, her hero; and a father filled with regret, guilt, and pain, clinging tightly to the apple of his eye. How long they would sit like this, it really didn't matter. For now, they had each other.

Watch Your Mouth!

•

This story is found in Judges, chapter 11.
The true characters are Jephthah and his unnamed daughter.

•

Have you as a parent sacrificed time with your child or children in the name of career, promotion, or even pride? They grow up fast, and once they have grown, we can never recapture their youth. Think very carefully the next time someone wants you to compromise or accept a certain position. Ask yourself these questions: What will it cost me in terms of my family? What are my motives for accepting?

Don't allow your past or your emotions to make decisions for you. Like the father in this story, you might live to regret it very much because sometimes the decisions you make today will not only affect you and your children now but also future generations to come. Pray and ask God to guide you to make right choices. Study His Word, and find your answer. Seek Him, and make the right decision even if it hurts.

Keep your heart with all diligence,
For out of it spring the issues of life.
(Proverbs 4: 23)

Chapter 11

Single, but Not Alone

Hortence heard her mistress's voice calling, "Hortence! Hortence! Come here at once!"

Rushing to her mistress's side, Hortence bowed, "Yes, mistress?"

"Sit down. Tonight, you will sleep in the master's tent."

•

The master and his wife had lived in Egypt for some time, and on their departure Hortence, being a native of Egypt, had joined them. Over the years the two women developed a complicated relationship. Sometimes the mistress shared personal thoughts with her – like the time when she confided that she wasn't sure whether their childless state was the master's fault or hers. Then at other times, it was strictly a mistress and servant relationship.

•

Hortence hoped her face did not betray her disbelief. "Me?" she asked timidly.

Single, but Not Alone

"It's a job like all the other jobs you do around here. Don't go getting any funny ideas. It is solely to produce an heir!"

Funny ideas? She's got to be kidding. What on earth possessed her to formulate such a plan? I've had my eyes on Carl as a husband for quite some time now. If I do this, I can kiss Carl goodbye!

The thought of sleeping with the master was not at all funny to Hortence. Okay, so he didn't quite look his age, and he was a bit rugged, but he sure wasn't Carl. Hortence reminded herself that as a slave she had no choice but to obey. Tonight she would sleep with the master under his tent and just pretend he was Carl.

•

Hortence soon discovered she was with child. The mistress moved her into her tent in order to "take care" of her. She was taking no chances. *What a change one night can bring to your life!* mused Hortence.

However, with each passing day, things grew more difficult between the two women, and as Hortence's stomach increased in size, so too did her mistress's distrust of her. To cap it all, Hortence did nothing to help the situation. Sometimes she just could not resist a little bit of haughtiness here and there; after all, she was a *woman*, and *all* woman at that. A slave she might be, but this slave was carrying the master's heir. Now it could be seen where the barrenness lay!

Somehow, Hortence did not realize she was treading a dangerous path. To incur the wrath of the mistress was not wise, even if she was carrying the master's heir. She had forgotten one small detail. Her mistress was still the wife,

Dollys Y Crooks

and nothing but death could alter that fact. She might be a barren wife, but she was still *the* wife.

•

One day, Hortence overheard the mistress complaining to the master, "Something has to be done about her. She is behaving above her station."

"Whatever you think best, dear," replied the master. "Do whatever makes you happy. She is your servant."

The master would do anything for a quiet life. How he wished his life would go back to some normalcy. Why had he ever agreed to his wife's plan? Of course he knew the answer – for a bit of peace!

Hortence's ears began to tingle. How could he say that? She was carrying his child, his heir. Suddenly, Hortence came down to earth with a bump. This was the woman he loved. Had he not loved her all these years, despite her barrenness? Why should anything change just because *she* was carrying his child? After all, she was merely a servant girl.

Hortence learnt a valuable lesson in humility that day, but alas, it was too late. The mistress, having obtained the master's permission, began to treat her harshly. It seemed to Hortence that no matter what she did, she was still despised in her mistress's eyes.

"I can't take this much longer. I've tried. It's no use. Whatever I do just doesn't seem to work," sighed Hortence. Unable to bear the situation any longer, she felt that running away would solve all her problems. Her first thought was to return to her homeland, but she decided against it.

Single, but Not Alone

Returning pregnant without a father would be too much shame to bear.

Before the sun rose, while everyone was still asleep, Hortence left with only a few provisions and headed south. Where she would end up was the least of her worries.

•

Alone and six months pregnant, Hortence found herself in a wilderness that held only fear and anxiety. Whatever happened, she must continue on her journey.

As the day drew to a close, unable to go any further, she stopped at a little cave dug out of the mountainside beside which was a fountain of water. She would be safe here tonight. Tomorrow she would travel onwards.

Preparing to settle down for the night, she suddenly heard a voice, "Hortence, where have you come from, and where are you going?"

Fear seized her heart. No one had been here when she arrived. Who knew her name? Who could it be? She was sure she'd been alone the whole time. Trembling, she turned to see a man standing to her right. As she looked into his face, her fear gave way to curiosity.

"Who are you? Where did you come from? How do you know my name?" Hortence asked. "I thought I was alone here."

"You ask too many questions," the stranger replied with a smile. "Now answer my questions. I asked first, remember."

His smile instantly put Hortence at ease. She was so pleased to have someone to talk to that she poured her heart out to him; her words intermingling with tears.

Dollys Y Crooks

Patiently, the stranger listened to her story without interrupting. When she had finished, he said, "Return to your mistress, and submit yourself once again. God has heard your cry and has seen your pain. You will bear a son, and his name shall mean 'God hears.' He will be a great man, and a nation shall come out of him."

Though they were words Hortence did not wish to hear, she knew in her heart that the stranger was right. His words had caused a peace to overshadow her pain and anguish. How could she possibly bring a child up this way? How would they survive? Yes, his words made sense. Smiling, Hortence thanked him and promised that she would do as he had said.

"No need to be afraid tonight," he said gently; "you'll be okay." Instantly, the stranger vanished.

Pondering her encounter with the stranger, Hortence concluded that an angel had visited her. She became aware that the Almighty God that she often saw and heard her master and mistress pray to was real. Although she had not prayed to Him, He had heard her inner cry. He'd seen her pain and sent His angel to comfort her. Tomorrow she would make the journey back and ask this God who had heard her inner cry to help her retrace her steps.

"Thank you, my master's and mistress's God," she whispered before sinking into a deep sleep.

•

Hortence returned and begged for her mistress's forgiveness. The mistress, having had time to reflect and being in a much calmer frame of mind, gave her another

Single, but Not Alone

chance. Hortence, for her part, became obedient in everything she was required to do.

•

Finally the day came, and she gave birth to a boy just as the stranger, her "angel," had said. She was overjoyed at his birth, and so, it seemed, was her mistress. The master too was happy. When the boy was old enough, the master carried him everywhere and taught him all he knew. Hortence, after her past experience, was always very careful to stay in the background and never to bring attention her way again. Life went on for the master's household at a peaceful rate, just as he had always wanted it to be.

•

However, when the boy was thirteen years old, something happened that changed everything. If Hortence thought having her son was a life-changing experience, she had yet to experience one that would be more painful than bringing him to birth.

One day, three strangers came to visit the master while Hortence and the mistress were in the tent. Hortence overheard one of them tell the master that his wife would have a son this time next year. The stranger's words brought fear to her heart. How could that be? *She's barren, not to mention the fact that she's also old and past childbearing age. My son is the heir! What will happen to us should these words come to pass?*

Hortence looked over at her mistress. Had she heard those same words too? She had indeed, for the mistress was

143

Dollys Y Crooks

smiling and looking straight at her. As their eyes met, her smile broke into laughter. Unlike Hortence, the stranger's words had brought joy to her mistress's heart.

Hortence turned away and quietly continued her chores. "That will never happen! She's barren and too old," she consoled herself in a whisper.

•

Though she thought it was impossible for her mistress to conceive, every now and then she sneaked a look at her. At one such time, Hortence reflected on her experience in the cave with the stranger she called her "angel." Hadn't she believed his word and returned to her mistress, and hadn't his word come to pass? What if the mistress believed this word too? Could it come to pass? Could she really have a child at *her* age?

Hortence did not have long to wait to find out. Soon, the mistress informed her household that she was indeed pregnant. The stranger's words came to pass exactly as he had said, and the mistress gave birth to a son. After all the years of suffering and torment, the mistress held her son, born from her own womb, in her aged and wrinkled arms.

Hortence congratulated her but couldn't help wondering what would become of her and her son. She knew in her heart that time was running out for them both. Even if they never made a mistake, the mistress would always find fault with them.

Fourteen years ago, she had returned and submitted herself again to her mistress. Life was okay, though occasionally the mistress would lapse into one of her jealous rages when it appeared that the master spent too much

Single, but Not Alone

time with the boy, who was a constant reminder of her barrenness.

Now that the mistress had her own son, she would no longer need to tolerate this elevated slave girl and her son, even if the boy was her husband's.

•

Soon after the mistress's son was weaned, Hortence's worst fears materialized. One day, her son jokingly teased the younger boy, and the mistress took great offence. She demanded that the master send them away. This was the last straw. How dare he make fun of *her* son?

Hortence could only watch as the master, head bowed, slowly walked to his tent. She heard him pleading with his God, the same One she'd become aware of in her wilderness experience, to intervene in this recurrent situation and give him a solution once and for all.

She wondered: if he had prayed fourteen years ago when the mistress came up with this plan, would she have married Carl and lived happily ever after? Sadly, Hortence shook her head and walked towards her own tent. What was done, was done. Her son was the best thing that came out of a bad idea.

Very early the next day the master came to the door of her tent with a morose look on his face. He had shared countless happy moments with his firstborn, and over the years they had bonded well. Now he clearly felt he had no choice but to let them go, for the sake of a peaceful household.

"I am so sorry, Hortence. It hurts me to see you and the lad go, but I have no alternative. The Almighty God whom

Dollys Y Crooks

I serve has given me His word that He will take care of you both. Here are some provisions for your journey."

Calling the young boy, his father and master kissed him and told him to take care of his mother. Then, sadly, he turned and walked away.

Hortence said goodbye to her mistress and, without a trace of malice in her voice, wished her well. Then, after bowing before her for the last time, she again set off in a southerly direction –only this time she was in the company of her teenage son.

•

Passing the cave again, she reflected on the past fourteen years. Then, she'd been with child; now she was holding the hands of that child, still unsure of her destination. *Funny how life has a way of taking you back to the same spot years later*, she said to herself. What to do now? They could only keep moving.

Moving from one barren place into the next, Hortence discovered that their provisions were running low. With the intense heat of the midday sun bearing down upon them, she gave her son the last drop of water and the remaining food. "If we have to die in this wilderness, at least we will die together," she told him sadly.

The thought of seeing her son slowly die became unbearable for her. She placed him in a clearing in a bush and then walked away as the child sobbed. When she thought she was distant enough not to see him but still able to hear him, she sat down under a small tree with a thousand "whys" flooding her mind.

Single, but Not Alone

After a while, Hortence wondered whether her son was still alive. She could hear no sound from his direction. Afraid to go and look, she thought of her "angel." Where was he? Could he see her now?

Suddenly she heard a familiar voice. "What's wrong, Hortence?"

She turned and smiled. He did see her.

"Please, rise and take care of your son. He is alive. God has heard his sobs. He can't die. Did I not tell you of the future that lies ahead for him? Don't you remember?"

Choked with emotion, Hortence replied, in a voice barely above a whisper, "I was wondering where you were, and yes, I do remember now what you told me. But how could that be? Look where we are now."

"Dry the tears from your eyes, and look ahead."

Obeying his instructions once more, Hortence saw a pool of water. Eagerly, she ran towards it, all the while shouting to her son. "There's water! There's water!"

It was indeed water, which quenches the throat of the thirsty and revives the spirit of the weary. Hortence held her son, close to collapsing, in her arms and wept.

Pouring water on the boy's parched lips, she cried, "You can't die. You simply can't die. What the angel told me about your birth came to pass. I have no reason to doubt him now."

The stranger's words at her first wilderness experience had brought her peace. Now, years later, in her second encounter, they brought her strength. Hortence deliberately bypassed all the negative thoughts that bombarded her mind and brought it instead to a place of tranquillity and quiet assurance. Through no fault of her own she had found

Dollys Y Crooks

herself in this situation, but it would be okay now. She had the promise of her "angel."

•

Her son and his descendants did indeed grow up to become a nation, just as the stranger had said. His people are still in existence today and are known as the Arab nation.

•

This story is found in Genesis, chapters 16, 18, and 21. The true characters are Abraham, Sarah, Hagar, and Ishmael.

•

Can you see yourself in this story? Are you in a wilderness through no fault of your own? Are you running away from your problems or, if you are a Christian, running back to the world and its system which you thought you had left behind? Has this Christian journey been too hard for you to bear? The people in the church you attend are mean and unfeeling! They are all a bunch of hypocrites! Are you leaving because the pastor and his wife are unaware that you exist? Is it because someone you trusted did this to you or said that about you?

Stop a while at the fountain, and talk to the One who gives the living water that enables us never to thirst again. Let Him refresh your soul. Ponder for a while, how did you come to know the Lord Jesus Christ? Who saved you? Was it the church or the pastor? It is only when we are honest

Single, but Not Alone

with ourselves and towards God that we begin to heal and see things the way He does.

Sometimes He tells us, as the angel did, "Return and submit yourself under their authority. It may be rough for a while, but I promise if you will be obedient to My word, I will do great and mighty things on your behalf!"

You see, it is in our obedience that He blesses us, and it is in our ability to remain focused on what He has called us to do that we receive the promise and the blessings that come with it.

Our wildernesses are not the same. They are all different, but we can be sure of one thing: when we place our *faith* in Him, He will give us a promise or a word to bring us through. He will open your eyes and cause you to see that your situation is not usually as bad as you think it is.

Just as He did not leave this young woman and her son alone in a wilderness that held fear and anxiety, neither will He leave you there. Regardless of your situation, know for sure that He will send help, direction, and sustenance just for you – even if He has to send an "angel" to do it.

When you pass through the waters, I will be with you;
And through the rivers, they shall not overflow you.
When you walk through the fire, you shall not be burned,
Nor shall the flame scorch you.
For I am the Lord *your God ....*
(Isaiah 43: 2–3)

Chapter 12

The Master Always Has a Plan!

The future looked glorious for Noreen, her husband, and their two sons as they migrated to a new land. She felt confident and happy in her husband Alvin's decision to leave their land of famine, especially since they were not getting any younger and had two strapping boys – Maurice, the elder, and Codero – to take care of.

•

Life in the new land was good. There was plenty to eat and drink, in contrast to their homeland, where many had lost a great deal in the famine. Noreen often wondered how her family and friends were back home, though they were few, for most had migrated to other countries just as they had. She had no wish to return to her homeland; life here was good, very good. The Almighty had indeed blessed her family. Alvin had recently opened up a nursery, selling exotic plants and unusual pottery. The children were both doing well, academically and socially. Noreen felt the

The Master Always Has a Plan!

Almighty had truly smiled on their decision to migrate. Did not her name mean "blessed?"

•

Then out of the blue, tragedy struck. Alvin died. Her husband of more than twenty years, whom she had loved from a young girl, was dead. The future now seemed utterly uncertain. How would she and the two boys survive? Just when everything was going so well, what had happened? Sadly, Noreen pulled Maurice out of college and had him run the family business full-time, with Codero helping after school.

Every now and then a tear would run down her cheek, and sadness intermingled with pain would cross her face as she thought of Alvin. The bed felt empty now that he wasn't there, and the only joy life held for her was her two sons. Each time Noreen looked at them, she thanked the Almighty for being merciful to her in not leaving her entirely alone. Codero especially reminded her of Alvin, for he had both his father's smile and many of his mannerisms.

How she missed Alvin! Would he still be alive if he hadn't opened the business? If he hadn't worked so hard, spending many hours making sure orders were completed and customers were kept satisfied? She had begged him often to come home early, but he would always reply, "Just have to complete this last order, honey, and I'll be home." It was always that last order. How could she complain when he was doing it for her and the boys? Maybe she should have been much firmer with him. So many "maybe" and "perhaps" thoughts ran though her mind. For now she would be

Dollys Y Crooks

grateful that the Almighty had not left her completely alone. She still had her sons, she reminded herself.

•

In time, both boys married women born from the land they now called home. Maurice married Ruth, and a few years later, Codero married Charlene. It was their custom to marry only within their culture, and Alvin would have surely sent the boys back to take wives, but since Noreen was a widow in a foreign land with a business to run, she couldn't afford to do that.

Noreen wished Alvin were around to see how happy the girls made his boys. They had grown to be fine young men, and now they were husbands too.

•

Noreen smiled as she remembered how Alvin used to teach them about Jehovah, the Almighty God of their forefathers, Abraham, Isaac, and Jacob. And oh, how the boys had loved to hear the stories of Moses, Joshua, Samson, and Joseph. They never grew tired of hearing them. Smiling again at those memories, Noreen looked forward to hearing those same stories being repeated in Alvin's absence to her grandchildren one day.

Once again life was good. Noreen was happy and contented. Her family circle had now expanded to include her two daughters-in-law. They were good girls, and again she looked forward to a day when grandchildren would be sitting on her knees singing the very songs she sang as a child on her grandmother's knees.

152

The Master Always Has a Plan!

•

Then, as if undeserving of so much joy, tragedy struck once again. This time, both her sons died when their car overturned on a dangerous bend on their way home from the business one evening. Noreen reeled in disbelief, her mind clothed in shock. "What have I done?" she asked in desperation. "Why is the Almighty's hand suddenly against me? It seems as if He blesses me only to curse me! Did I do the right thing in allowing Maurice and Codero to marry foreign wives? Is this the reason for their deaths?" She continued to ask these questions as the day drew near for the funeral of her sons.

Noreen stood at the burial ground wracked with guilt and pain as the plain caskets that contained her sons' bodies wrapped in simple linen shrouds were lowered into the ground. For the first time since leaving her homeland, the question of returning home came to the forefront of her mind.

There had been no need to ask such questions when life was good. It was only now, when it had been interrupted and cast into turmoil, that her mind turned to her homeland. She had heard the famine had ended some years ago and that the land was back to normality.

An exhausted Noreen returned home to grieve. What was left for her now in this foreign land? She felt completely alone.

•

A new day dawned, and Noreen awoke making a mental note of her situation. No husband, no children, not even

Dollys Y Crooks

grandchildren; only her memories, two daughters-in-law, and a lovely big home filled with an abundance of material possessions. Those and the home she would share equally between the girls, and the business she would sell to be able to support herself once she returned home.

"Yes," Noreen sighed, "I think it's time to return home." Whatever happened to the Almighty? Over the years, she had known Him as Jehovah Jireh (her Provider) but right now she needed Him to be her Jehovah Shalom (her Peace) and her Jehovah Rophi (her Healer). "God, where are you?" Noreen asked. "I feel so terribly alone."

She climbed out of bed, showered and dressed, and then held conference with Ruth and Charlene. With a heavy heart she informed them of her decision to return to her homeland. She told them she would leave the home with all its contents to share between them. Noreen thanked them for the times they had filled her, her sons, and her home with happiness and wished them well for the future.

It was a sad, lonely, and tired Noreen that rose from the table that day and proceeded to pack the little she would take for her journey home. Her memories would be enough for an old widow, left all alone, without a future to look forward to. Life, she reasoned, could be cruel. It gave you pleasures on one hand; then once you were accustomed to them, with the other hand, it simply took them away.

Unknown to Noreen, the girls had discussed with each other what would happen to them were they to remain. Had they not married foreigners? While their husbands were alive, they had their protection and a mother-in-law whose love they had reciprocated, enabling them to cope

The Master Always Has a Plan!

with the rejection and sneers they experienced from a few small-minded people.

Both girls concluded that life with their mother-in-law, in her homeland, might be a lot better than remaining in theirs.

Noreen, so engrossed in her thoughts, did not realize both girls had entered the room.

"Take us with you," they pleaded softly.

Upon hearing their voices, Noreen looked up, turned and said, "No, the Almighty's hand is against me. If you come with me, I can't promise you the standard of life you are used to here. I don't know what the future holds, and I don't want to be responsible for anything that might happen to you both."

•

Refusing to give up, the girls continued pleading, but Noreen was steadfast in her decision. Charlene knew that determined look and decided to take her chances, remain in her homeland, and hope one day to find someone who didn't care that she was once married to a foreigner.

However, Ruth decided to try once more. "I am not leaving you," she said with a determination that Noreen had never seen in her before. "Where you go, I will go, and where you choose to live, so will I. Your God shall become my God, and where you die, so will I. That I promise you."

How could she leave this woman who'd been there for her every time there was a need? Through every situation and problem, Ruth could always count on Noreen. Mother-in-law and daughter-in-law, old and young, Jew and

Dollys Y Crooks

non-Jew, widows together – whatever the future held, she was convinced they could face it together.

•

The day came for Noreen and Ruth to leave. As the women set off on their long journey, Charlene's tears were flowing. She kissed them both and thanked Noreen for her kindness towards her during the years she had been married to Codero. Then she asked Ruth to take good care of Noreen and to keep in touch. Finally, she waved goodbye and entered the lovely big house filled with an abundance of material things. What would she do now? Where would she begin?

•

With very few belongings, Noreen and Ruth approached the gate to the city of Noreen's hometown. They had returned at the height of barley harvest. The whole town would be out, and news of her return would spread quickly. There was no sneaking back to the old house now. Fear gripped Noreen's heart, and her steps became unsteady. Ruth gently put an arm around her mother-in-law and whispered, "Don't worry, let's keep going. We've come too far to turn back."

At the sight of Noreen, people came rushing out of their houses. They came out to see the woman they had heard of who had left with everything and was now returning with very little. Some were still alive who had told her and Alvin they were making a big mistake; they felt gratified as they saw her walking no longer uprightly but with a slight stoop.

The Master Always Has a Plan!

Though they did not actually voice their opinion, their faces said it all.

Young children had not known her but had heard of the rich landowner whose big house stood empty. They asked questions like "Mummy, is this the lady who has the big empty house? Where is her husband, and where are her children?"

Others whispered loud enough for her to hear, "Noreen has returned with a foreigner. Only foreigners we have around here are servants, but *she* doesn't look like one. We heard Noreen let her sons marry them foreign women; perhaps this is one of them. Weren't our girls good enough for her sons then?"

It seemed to Noreen that very few were happy that she had returned home.

In an effort to close their mouths and get on with the task of rebuilding her life, Noreen decided to set the record straight from the beginning. As she opened her mouth to speak, everyone fell silent. Seeing she had gained their attention, Noreen said with all the force she could muster up:

"I could tell you it's none of your business, and I would be right. Yes, I left full, rich, and blessed. Now you see me poor and empty. Please allow me to introduce my daughter-in-law, this foreigner, as you call her. Her name, if you please, is Ruth. Now, kindly make way so that we may get on with rebuilding our lives. By the way, if it makes you feel any better, why don't you call me "Carolyn" (meaning "bitter") rather than Noreen? Good day to you all!"

Pulling herself up to her full stature and lifting her head high, Noreen headed for the front door of her empty home.

Dollys Y Crooks

"That's put paid to all their prejudices and innuendos," she angrily told Ruth.

•

At the front door to Noreen's home, this home she had not seen in many years, she hesitated. Ruth sensed the older woman's anxiety and stood quietly by her side, saying and doing nothing. Finally, Noreen gently pushed the door open. Having entered, she went from room to room, with Ruth beside her. Then, as if giving a guided tour, she gushed, "This room was where my husband brought me after the consummation of our marriage, and this room is where the children were born." Exiting through the back door, Noreen's tour continued. "This yard was where all the celebrations were held; every birthday, every event happened here."

Eventually, an exhausted Noreen sat down and wept uncontrollably. The grief and guilt she had felt these past months came gushing out in her tears like a river overflowing its bank. They were too strong to suppress any longer. Ruth could only sit silently with her arms around her mother-in-law. This moment, she knew was, a private one, a healing one for the woman she had grown to love and admire these past years.

Ever since the death of Noreen's sons, Ruth had tried several times to get her to share her grief and pain, but it was no use. Seeing her now was like ointment being poured upon a wound, which Ruth knew would take no time at all to heal. Finding a blanket, Ruth gently laid it over her mother-in-law. Tomorrow would be another day.

The Master Always Has a Plan!

It is surprising how some decisions you make in life can take you away and then bring you back to the very place you left, only to start all over again – this time older and hopefully a bit wiser.

•

The women spent the next few days cleaning and putting the house in order. Then their thoughts turned to ways of providing for themselves since the proceeds from the nursery were not yet finalised and the sustenance they had brought with them was nearly spent. Noreen was too old to work, so it fell to Ruth. But what could she do?

Noreen told Ruth of a custom her people had. It was known as "gleaning" and was a means of ensuring that the poor, the stranger, and those who had fallen on hard times would still be able to eat. The poor could follow the reapers at harvest time, collecting and consuming any crops that might fall to the ground or be left behind. Eagerly, Ruth's eyes lit up, she would do this gleaning and keep them both from starving.

Early the next day, Ruth set out and found a field. She worked hard following after the reapers. Unbeknownst to her, the field she worked in belonged to a rich landowner who was a relative of her deceased father-in-law.

Mr. Daryl had just returned from a visit away and decided to check how things were going in his field. He came across Ruth and saw that she was a stranger, so he enquired of his manager who she was.

"That's the foreign woman who came with Alvin's widow" was the reply. "She has been here from early morning and only stopped to eat once. I tell you one thing, sir: she

Dollys Y Crooks

sure is a hard worker. If our reapers worked like her, this field would be finished in no time at all!"

Daryl laughed and called her over. "Stay in my field," he said. "I have commanded my young men not to trouble you. When you need a drink, take it from one of the vessels they have filled."

Ruth bowed graciously and thanked him for all his kindness towards her. Then she boldly asked him why he had paid such attention to her. Was it because she was a foreigner and had stood out?

"No," he replied. "I have heard of your kindness to your mother-in-law in leaving your homeland after the death of your husband and returning with her to our land, where our customs and practices are strange to you. I pray that our God under whose wings you have come to trust will repay you for such faith."

Ruth thanked him again. Only this time, she smiled. Passing her some parched corn, Daryl returned the compliment.

As Ruth resumed her gleaning, Daryl commanded his men to let handfuls of crops purposely drop to the ground for her to gather up.

What a day this has been! Ruth said to herself. *I wonder what will happen tomorrow?* She couldn't wait to get home and tell Noreen all about her day, but first she must beat this grain out, or else there wouldn't be any supper tonight.

•

Meanwhile, Noreen was at home still trying to digest the change in her circumstances and wondering how Ruth's day was going. "It must surely be time for her to return now,"

The Master Always Has a Plan!

she said anxiously. No sooner had she spoken those words than the door burst open, and in came a flushed and excited Ruth whose rush of words made no sense at all to Noreen.

"Now calm down and tell me all about your day. Where did you glean?"

Ruth showed Noreen the amount of barley she had beaten out of the grain she had gleaned.

Noreen exclaimed, "Blessed is the man that took notice of *you* today. Who was he? What's his name?"

The tables were turned. Ruth wondered who needed calming down now.

When all the excitement had subsided and both women were much calmer, Noreen realized that the man was a relative of her deceased husband. Daryl came from good stock and was one of the few who had remained and survived the famine. He had refused to leave, trusting that the Almighty was able to provide for all his needs, including those of his business. God did not disappoint, and Daryl had indeed prospered during the famine.

Knowing this, Noreen advised her daughter-in-law to do as he had said, for he meant well. Ruth had no qualms about accepting her advice. She had proven Noreen to be a wise woman in times past.

As Noreen reflected over the day's events, a slight ray of hope pierced the darkness around her. The Almighty might after all have a plan and a purpose behind the pain and grief she had gone through these past years, but what?

For the first time in a long while, Noreen knelt and prayed. She thanked the Almighty for not forgetting her, even though she had blamed Him for her husband's and sons' deaths. She asked Him to bless Ruth for her faithfulness and

Dollys Y Crooks

courage in leaving her homeland to accompany her back to hers. She thanked Him for the kindness He had shown to her through Ruth's presence. Concluding her prayer with "Amen," Noreen, excited about what the future might hold, climbed into bed and fell asleep straight away. This was not a night for insomnia.

•

Shortly after, Noreen had the joy of seeing her prayers answered. Ruth went on to marry Daryl, the rich landowner – the man who had shown such kindness to her, the foreigner. Respect was now given to both Noreen and her daughter-in-law. Was not the hand of the Almighty on them, and were not His blessings now plain for all to see?

The couple then went on to have a son who nourished and restored the faith of a widow in the One who she thought had dealt her a harsh and bitter blow. For she later came to realize that He had used her trials to work out His purpose.

•

This story is found in Ruth.
The true characters are Naomi; her husband, Elimelech;
their sons, Mahlon and Chilion, and daughters-in-law,
Ruth and Orpah; and the rich landowner, Boaz.

•

You may, like this widow, have had everything, then one day something went drastically wrong. You had to file for bankruptcy; your marriage was dissolved and now you feel you have nothing. *Wrong!* You have so much to live for. You

The Master Always Has a Plan!

have life, hope, and faith. Cling to them, and put them to work for you. Just as Ruth was an encourager in her mother-in-law's life when things got rough, God will send you an encourager too.

When life seems tough, and God is nowhere to be found, don't give up. He *is* there. Perhaps you can't see Him, but that doesn't mean He is not around. He has promised never to leave you, neither to forsake you, when you put your faith in Him. You must believe that He is working things out for your good.

God is not mentioned in the story of Ruth, but His loving care and infinite mercy can be seen throughout. Ruth did not just "happen" to find herself in the rich man's field - God ordered her steps there.

You see, we never go through anything just for ourselves. Noreen's life had to be turned upside down in order for her foreign daughter-in-law to become part of the ancestry of Jesus Christ. David, Israel's greatest king and writer of most of the Psalms we read and love so well, was her great-grandson.

Hold tight! Be patient. If you will continue in *faith*, in time, you too will know the purpose for your adversities. You too will understand that despite whatever comes against you, the Master *always* has a plan!

> *And we know that all things work together*
> *for good to those who love God, to those who*
> *are the called according to His purpose.*
> *(Romans 8: 28)*

> *God bless.*

Heavenly Father

I thank You for those that You have drawn
by Your Spirit to read this book.
I pray that they would allow You,
The Master of every trial, pain,
and heartache that has already come or will
come their way, to mould and fashion them.

Isaiah 64: 8 states
"But now, O Lord, You are our Father;
We are the clay, and You our potter;
And we are all the work of Your hand."

Father, take us, mould us, breathe afresh on us,
and cause us to know that You
have *all* things under control.
Help us understand that when we place
our lives into Your hand,
You can do with them as You please for
You are the One that has redeemed us,
paid the price, and set us free.

And Daddy, when all is said and done,
You get the glory, and our lives are
enriched by the very things we go through.
Then when we have been strengthened, we become
beacons of light and hope to those who are
treading the same path we once took.

Thank You for loving us and taking the time
to perfect us into the image of
Your dear Son,
Jesus Christ.
Amen!

The Author would very much welcome your feedback.
www.masterpiecesofthemaster.co.uk